"Rhys's last letter.
Read it yourself."

Raoul tossed the letter onto the table. Dell continued to look at him coldly.

"No?" he continued. "Well, I'll tell you then." He picked up the letter and quoted "'...As God is my witness, she is driving me to madness!'"

"Me!" Shock waves sounded in Dell's voice. "Does Rhys mention me by name?"

"He doesn't have to. It's you all right. 'My fiancée'...he says it quite clearly. I'm sorry you ever came here. You, the person he loved and trusted— the person who betrayed him!"

"Raoul, it's not what it appears," she protested. "It wasn't me."

But Dell knew Raoul didn't believe her. And she couldn't think of any way to convince him....

WELCOME
TO THE WONDERFUL WORLD
OF *Harlequin Presents*

Interesting, informative and entertaining,
each Harlequin romance portrays an appealing
and original love story. With a varied array
of settings, we may lure you on an African safari,
to a quaint Welsh village, or an exotic Riviera
location—anywhere and everywhere that adventurous
men and women fall in love.

As publishers of Harlequin romances, we're
extremely proud of our books. Since 1949,
Harlequin Enterprises has built its publishing
reputation on the solid base of quality and
originality. Our stories are the most popular
paperback romances sold in North America; every
month, six new titles are released and sold at
nearly every book-selling store in Canada and the
United States.

A free catalogue listing all available Harlequin romances
can be yours by writing to the

HARLEQUIN READER SERVICE,
(In the U.S.) M.P.O. Box 707, Niagara Falls, N.Y. 14302
(In Canada) Stratford, Ontario, Canada N5A 6W2

We sincerely hope you enjoy reading
this Harlequin Presents.

Yours truly,

THE PUBLISHERS

ABRA TAYLOR

lost mountain

Harlequin Books

TORONTO · LONDON · NEW YORK · AMSTERDAM
SYDNEY · HAMBURG · PARIS · STOCKHOLM

Harlequin Presents edition published February 1980
ISBN 0-373-10342-5

Original hardcover edition published in 1979
by Mills & Boon Limited

CHAPTER ONE

'You have to be married to your job,' her uncle had said. He had said it four years before, when Dell Everett had first joined his publishing firm; and he had said it again, recently, before sending her off on this strange expedition into the heart of France.

You have to be married to your job. And those were the words that had embroiled her, once again, in the lie that had governed her life for this past year; the lie that had tied her, in the public's mind at least, to the well-known name of Rhys Morgan; the lie she thought she had laid to rest with Rhys Morgan's ashes ...

Dell shivered a little in recollection, and pulled her coat closer about her—but perhaps it was only the late-spring chill in the windswept railway station where the French train had so recently deposited her. The thin clear mountain air was invigorating here in the wild north-eastern reaches of the Massif Central, but the woollen coat Dell wore, a tawny beige that set off the golden auburn of her hair, was too light for the rarefied atmosphere. All the same she preferred to wait outside the smoke-filled station house, where four dour old Auvergnats had been arguing over an incomprehensible card game.

Against the wall of the station house, the wind flapped at a weathered sign. *Saint-Just-sur-Haute vous invite*, it began; but the rest of its message was obscured

5

by age. To the north lay the village that had issued the invitation. It slept in the cool spring sunshine, a cluster of small, crooked houses wearing time like a signature. Ridged red-tiled roofs climbed the mountain like stepping stones, and the lichened walls seemed to grow out of the volcanic rock. A squat stone wall surrounded the entire village.

The Massif Central ... Rhys had sometimes written about this country. It had been in his blood, at least in the French half of his blood. Puy-de-Dôme, the Cantals, the Margeride, Aveyron and the Gorges du Tarn, the soft Cévennes and the fertile Haute Loire ... Now, faced with these purple spines of mountains that ridged their way down across a fifth of the land mass of France, Dell had a sense of *déjà vu*. This was a land she had seen before, not with her eyes but with her heart, through Rhys Morgan's poetry.

Rhys Morgan. The name conjured up the face. Suddenly Dell had a vision of him: his ghost silently laughing at her, a dark lock of hair falling over his handsome, undisciplined face, just as he had sometimes laughed at her when he was alive.

Rhys Morgan, who had been her fiancé in name only. How had she ever allowed her uncle to talk her into the charade a year ago? But with no family beyond her uncle, and with no particular interest in the casual impermanent affairs indulged in by so many of her generation, Dell had indeed been married to her job in the publishing house. Partly, this had been the result of a genuine interest in and aptitude for the work; partly the result of a fierce loyalty to the uncle who, along with her aunt, had raised her for all those years after her parents' death.

Rhys Morgan had been one of the stable of writers to whom Dell had been assigned. The poetry he wrote, if not the man, had stirred her. Rhys, for his part, had come to depend on Dell's judgment; their relationship, after a few desultory passes on Rhys' part, had remained platonic.

There had never been any need for Rhys to pursue Dell, or in fact any woman who failed to succumb to his charms. For Rhys, there had always been women —hordes of women. The darkly handsome Welsh looks he had inherited from his father, and his reported sexual prowess, had made certain of that. Then, when his unashamedly erotic poetry had brought him fame, women had thrown themselves at him in a sort of frenzied ritual of hero-worship, seeing him in the rôle of a latter-day Dylan Thomas. The fact that Rhys had been a love-child himself, and his mother a celebrated French actress, had only added to the legend.

The sham engagement between Dell and Rhys Morgan had been undertaken at her uncle's behest, to protect Rhys from himself, and from his reputation as a womaniser. On that last lecture tour across the United States, it had been important to keep Rhys out of trouble as far as possible; the schedule had been a heavy one, and Rhys was only too easily led astray. Dell, reluctantly, had agreed to the deception. As for Rhys, he too had been willing to go along with the charade. He had found it useful for fending off women whose attentions he found unwelcome, while in no way restricting him in dalliances of his own choosing.

For a time it had seemed that her uncle's judgment had been right. Dell's presence on the lecture tour, and her supposed engagement to Rhys, had indeed kept some of the female scalp-hunters away from her famous and unstable charge. At least until the end ...

But how was she to know that Rhys had not even told his own mother the true state of affairs? Dell had thought the deception dead, like Rhys—and then the letter had arrived, bearing its French stamp and blurred postmark, and it had begun all over again. Rhys' mother had written to Wilfred Everett to suggest that his niece, and only his niece, come to stay for a time in the Massif Central, and sift through the sheaves of unpublished poetry and other papers that Rhys had parcelled home over the years. She would not agree to shipping the poetry to England. She would not agree to the sending of a substitute editor in Dell's place. She did not seem to care whether the poetry was published or not; she had no need of money. She wanted to meet her dead son's fiancée, and if the fiancée would not come, then no one was to come.

'But I can't!' Dell had said to her uncle, two weeks before with a hot sting of colour in her cheeks. 'Imagine what she'll think of me! Especially since Rhys dedicated that last volume of poetry to me—and you know how explicit *that* was.'

'We all know he wasn't writing about you,' her uncle had said affably. 'Frankly, I think Rhys found you refreshing after all those female sycophants—and you did help him prepare the book for publication. That's why he dedicated it to you.'

'His mother doesn't know that. She'll think it's for —well, other reasons. She's sure to believe I'm a loose woman.'

Wilfred Everett had thrown back his leonine head and laughed. 'Eugénie de Briand is the last person to worry about loose women! Her affair with Rhys Morgan's father was the most celebrated affair of its decade! The great French actress who abandoned her husband, her career, her young son, everything, all for the love of a struggling Welsh playwright ... no, she won't think you're a loose woman.'

'But there's the rest of the family,' Dell had protested.

'What rest of the family? She lives alone in a château in the Auvergne. It's years since she's been in the public eye, and I understand she's something of a recluse. Go on, Dell, you'll be doing her a favour. She's a lonely woman who wants to meet the girl her son loved.'

'The girl she thinks he loved,' muttered Dell; but she had agreed, with misgivings, to go.

And so she had been swept back into this deception that went against the grain ...

'Mademoiselle Everett?' The voice, French-accented, grated from somewhere behind her, and Dell swung around with a smile of relief, knowing it would be the chauffeur she had been told to expect.

The smile was not returned, and she felt her own die on her lips. There was no hint of welcome in the face that towered several inches above her; only a look of raw dislike. For a moment she felt off balance, dwarfed by the man's presence, even though she was a tall girl herself. It took a few seconds before she recovered her wits.

'Are you Madame de Briand's chauffeur?' She forced a stiff smile back to her lips. Perhaps she was only imagining that cold disapproval in his eyes. Dark purplish-black eyes, Dell noted with some corner of her mind, the colour of the lava stone in these regions.

At her question, the frown that bracketed his mouth only deepened. He made no effort to answer her. Instead, he flicked his eyes impatiently over her slender figure and the rather unpractical travelling suit she had worn in order to look presentable for Madame de Briand. His eyes lingered on the two suitcases at her feet, evidence of the protracted stay that would be required in order to go through all of Rhys' papers.

Dell tried to swallow the sense of discomfort he had stirred in her. Now, with his eyes no longer staring her down, she allowed herself a closer look at the man who had been sent to meet her. There was something in his face that reminded her of the mountains that lumped behind him—something primitive and elemental. It was a craggy face, gaunt about the cheekbones, not particularly good-looking. Dell sensed that he was in his mid-thirties, perhaps ten or twelve years older than herself. His hair was a little too long, and whipped into black disorder by the chill breeze. Beneath it, the forbidding slash of his brows was a disturbing reminder of the fact that the next few weeks were a question mark in her life. Madame de Briand had seemed touchingly eager to have Dell stay; but would the rest of the household consider her visit an imposition?

The man had still not answered her initial question, and Dell realised she should have put it to him in French. So she repeated: 'Vous êtes le chauffeur de Madame de Briand?'

'Venez avec moi,' the man returned curtly, without answering her question directly. With that he swept up the larger of her suitcases quite effortlessly, and strode off along the station platform without so much as a glance to see if she was following. Dell tightened her lips with a surge of annoyance, for the suitcase he had left behind was, although smaller, by far the heavier of the two, and she already had a small carry-all over her shoulder in addition to her purse. What a way for a chauffeur to behave!

'If he worked for me I'd fire him,' she muttered to herself as she heaved at the remaining suitcase and hurried after him. Well, perhaps it was hard to hire a decent chauffeur here in the Auvergne. And even making allowances for the ruggedness of the setting, he was hardly dressed properly for the job. He wore shapeless patched trousers and an ancient brown leather jacket that had long since passed its prime—a day labourer's outfit similar to those worn by the old men inside the railway station. Perhaps he also did some of the heavy work around Madame de Briand's place? Certainly, his rangy hard-shouldered frame looked capable of it. She hoped his brusque manner was not typical of the rest of the household staff. If so, she had an uncomfortable few weeks ahead of her.

The man's stride was long, and Dell started a half-run to keep up with him. On the rough surface of ground beyond the railway station, she stumbled against a loose rock and twisted her ankle painfully. At that moment the man came to a halt beside a battered Renault of uncertain age, and turned back to watch her progress. Dell, recovering her balance, caught her lip at the near loss of dignity. She straightened herself as best she could and walked the rest of the distance with slow deliberation, fighting the twinge of pain and silently cursing the totally unpractical footwear she had chosen to wear today.

By the time she reached the car he had stowed the larger suitcase and was standing with the door on the passenger side open for her. Normally, Dell would have shrugged her shoulders and jumped into the front seat quite willingly. But the man's manners were intolerable; and she was angered by the fact that he had failed to relieve her of the rest of the luggage even after seeing her near fall.

'I'll sit in the back,' she stated firmly, forgetting for the moment the language barrier.

There was no response. It seemed that the man understood no English at all. And although Dell would have been willing to try her rusty French on anyone else, she wanted to display no more weaknesses in front of this antagonistic Frenchman. So she thrust her smaller suitcase into the space he had expected her to occupy, opened the rear door with a vicious jerk, and climbed in.

With that the man slammed the passenger door shut and went around to the driver's seat, without troubling to close the rear door behind Dell. She gasped at his insolence; prickles of resentment rose along the nape of her neck. She pulled the door closed and settled on to the rear seat, pushing aside an old afghan that lay on the worn upholstery and depositing her carry-all beside it angrily.

The man had settled into the front seat now, but he had made no move to start the car. Dell could see his knuckles whitening in his lap; he seemed to be trying to rein in some burst of temper. Surely he was not angry just because she had spoken to him in English?

It had been an honest oversight. And what was he waiting for now—an apology?

Well, he would get none from her, as long as he continued to be so rude. All the same, she must ask him to start the car; for a moment she cast about in her mind for the satisfactory French, without finding it. Finally she said : '*Je suis prête.*'

For answer, he flicked the ignition with a twist of lean brown fingers and slid the shift into reverse. His face, as he glanced over his shoulder to back the car, was etched with disapproval. Dell hoped he hadn't taken the cue for his manners from his mistress. Oh lord, why hadn't she taken the trouble to find out more about Madame de Briand! There was no point in making a scene over this man's boorish behaviour; it was a bad way to start a visit to a new country. All the same, perhaps she could exact a small measure of revenge, and he would never know.

'You—are—a—rude—horrible—insolent—impossible—peasant,' she said in a perfectly clear voice, in as sweet a tone as she could manage. It was childish, stupid, of course; but at least it gave her a safety valve for the temper she could feel rising within her.

He made no sign of having heard, and Dell allowed herself a small smile of vengeful amusement. The car bumped heavily through the cobbled streets of Saint-Just-sur-Haute. Dell relaxed, marvelling that the town had retained such a mediaeval quality, an island of time in the press of the twentieth century. Rhys had once said that the heart of France had retired to the Massif Central; it might well be true.

And this man who drove the car—he, too, might have stepped from a page in a mediaeval history book.

One of those cruel border lords, hawk on wrist, coldly surveying the purple distance to see what mediaeval keep might be plundered next—a predatory feudal prince, swooping down to take his toll from passing pilgrims. It was a strange image, and her mind must be wandering, Dell decided. More likely she ought to envisage him as a peasant of the mountains, clad in worn leathers and tending a mangy cow or some thin, ragged goats; sleeping in his one-room cottage with the pigs and chickens.

The second vision seemed less appropriate to the man, but she decided it was nevertheless more satisfactory. If the man must be put in a mental pigeonhole, she preferred not to think of him as a mediaeval lord. He didn't deserve it.

But why was she thinking about him at all? She tugged her eyes away from the line of hair that curled darkly over the time-rusted brown of his jacket. Now the car had passed beyond the walls of Saint-Just-sur-Haute. To one side dense woodlands of beech and oak rose defiantly up the slopes, their greens so deep they almost vanished into purple. To the other side, on a more gentle slope, lay a green pasture land patched with juttings of bedrock. A peasant with a mournful moustache plodded home behind a tawny red cow.

The road was becoming rougher now, twisting as it skirted the edges of the mountain. Hedges straggled their branches over the edge of the road. Occasionally the car would slice between rough rock walls where clumps of broom hung precariously, pockmarking the steep surfaces. In patches of clearing where the vegetation thinned or the rock dropped away Dell could see the rolling scrubby meadows of the verdant highland.

Suddenly the car turned off the main road into a single track. Ahead lay a twisted rise of road and a towering crest of rock—the harsh lava rock of these volcanic hills, jutting with indigo ferocity in an assault against the sky.

Now Dell could see a château rising from the summit of the mountain, a dark solid structure still far in the distance. By this time her earlier annoyance at the driver had evaporated to some extent; at the moment, curiosity was a stronger motive than anger. Nevertheless, she chose her words carefully, unwilling to lay herself open to scorn for her poor command of French.

'*Est-ce que c'est le château-là?*'

'Very observant of you.' The reply was so sarcastic, so unexpected that Dell was startled into a state of near-shock. She flushed furiously. He could speak English! And yet he had let her make a complete, utter, unmitigated fool of herself!

Who was he, anyway? Obviously the man spoke more than a little English. A Frenchman with mere grammar-school command of the language might have said 'yes', even 'that's right', or 'correct'. But *very observant of you!* In that sardonic tone of voice! Dell wished the mountain would open and swallow her into some quiet chasm.

'Look, I'm sorry I called you rude.' After the first wave of shock had washed over her, Dell had found her voice. 'You should have told me you spoke English.'

'Why should I?'

'I can't think why you shouldn't. Unless you wanted me to make a fool of myself.'

'You can manage that without my help.' His voice was deliberately discourteous.

'Just what is that supposed to mean? I can't believe you're really a chauffeur or you wouldn't talk like this.'

After a moment's silence in which he failed to respond to her implied question, she went on: 'Do you work at the château or not?'

'Part of the time,' he said curtly, and nothing in his answer invited further questioning.

'What do you do?'

'Is that any of your business?'

Dell gaped furiously at the back of his head. How dare the man be so uncivil! True, her own words, earlier, had been ill-considered, but he had really called that upon himself. She had apologised. Yet he seemed determined to convey his contempt for her with every sentence he uttered. Dell had never been one to let anyone run roughshod over her, and she had no intention of starting now.

In a voice as controlled as she could manage under the circumstances, she returned: 'Of course it's my business. As I shall be a house guest for some time, I expect I shall come into contact with all the staff, including you, even though your job is only part-time. I'm not interested in what you do, only in how I can manage to avoid you. I shouldn't like to have to complain to Madame de Briand about your behaviour.'

'Nor should I,' came the blunt retort, 'about yours.'

Dell glared daggers at the back of his head, enraged by this dark man with his ill manners. His broad shoulders, hunched tensely against the seams of his worn jacket, told her that he was no more relaxed than she. And from the way that his fingers curled tightly around the steering wheel she wondered if he was making an effort to control some inner rage. What reason had he to dislike her so? What a ghastly man! Who was he? Not a chauffeur, she was sure by now. Not a gardener; his fingernails were too clean and well-kept. Perhaps his duties included other things ... Madame de Briand's business manager, perhaps? A job like that might be only part-time. But no: he was far too unpolished for that kind of work, and he looked as though he spent considerable time in the open air. Who *was* he? And why should she let his ill-bred remark pass unnoticed?

'Are you always this rude?' Dell said coldly. 'I can't believe you speak to your mistress the way you've spoken to me, or Madame de Briand would never employ you. Frankly, I think your attitude is quite uncalled-for.'

'Mademoiselle,' he replied acidly, 'as you're not my *mistress*, and not likely to be, I don't give a damn what you think.'

Dell, conscious of his intended insolence and the double meaning of his words, went pink to the roots of her hair. She bit back an angry retort. She would not give him the satisfaction of showing that she found his remark unsettling. Mistress indeed! Perhaps the man did have mistresses—this kind of male with his crude animal magnetism and his abrasive masculinity always appealed to *some* unfortunate woman. But how dared he imply that she, under any circumstances, might be a candidate for the position! Choking with indignation, she smothered her thoughts between clenched lips, and turned her attention back to the window, and the château that now loomed ahead.

It sat on the rock solidly, almost like another outcropping of the mountain itself—as indeed it was, in a way, for like most of the buildings in this part of the Massif Central, it was constructed of dark lava stone. It clung to the slope in steep and splendid solitude. The rigid rectangularity of its walls was interrupted by the curve of four round towers, one at each of the corners. These towers, with their red-tiled conical caps, made the structure look quite mediaeval. For a fleeting moment Dell had the peculiar sensation of sliding backwards in time, to days when a man like this might keep a lady walled within the castle keep ...

What a foolish thought! By the time the car had wound its way up the ribbon of road to the château, she had managed to recover some, if not all, of her aplomb. A quick rummage in her capacious handbag had produced the usual complement of feminine refreshers—lipstick, a comb, a small travel towelette to wipe the travel stains, if not the flush of embarrassment, from her face. Then a touch of perfume—but facing Madame de Briand would still be difficult. Especially now. Dell still felt at a disadvantage after her brief crossing of swords with this strange man.

The road twisted up to a solid stone entrance and through into a level cobbled courtyard. To the right was a grouping of outbuildings—large, gloomy stone stables, utilitarian but uninviting; a newer garage; a small shed; a gatekeeper's house. Watering troughs and heavy black metal hitching posts, curiously cast in gargoyle forms, stood near the stable door. In the centre of the courtyard was a stone-rimmed fountain. To the left stood the château itself, brooding over the heights like a stone giant, enduring, patient, massive, pitted but unperturbed by the passage of time and the siege of many winters. Many of its windows were mere slits, relics of an era when glass was unpractical and expensive.

The car sputtered, coughed ominously, and squeaked to a halt in front of the flagstone steps that led to the entrance. Dell's driver muttered a soft imprecation below his breath. Dell hesitated as he stepped out and walked around the car; for a moment it seemed he was going to make a gesture of common politeness and open the rear door of the car for her. Instead, he opened the boot and removed her luggage.

Dell sat for a moment, viewing him with cold distaste as he transferred the baggage to the front door of the château. What possible reason could Madame de Briand have for wanting such a discourteous man on her staff!

As if to dispel Dell's doubts about the reception that awaited her, the heavy oak door swung open and a squat plain woman emerged in a flurry of white apron. Her square face was creased in smiles. She hurried down the steps and opened the rear door of the car, leaning in and greeting Dell with a welcoming warmth of outstretched arms.

'Mademoiselle Everett! *Soyez la bienvenue!* I am Ernestine ... the 'ousekeeper of Madame de Briand. She has been listening for your arrival. The car is late, *non*? You have been waiting at the station for a time?'

'Yes, but not too long. All the same, I'm glad to be here—and delighted to meet you, Ernestine.'

'*Enfin*, you must be tired, *non*? I have prepared your room and the fire is burning there even this moment. You will see it now? Freshen, per'aps? Then I take you to Madame de Briand.'

The woman's warmth was infectious and Dell smiled gratefully in return, her cheeks curving into the suggestion of a dimple. 'Thank you, Ernestine, that would be lovely.'

Already the man had vanished with her luggage. Dell felt a twinge of annoyance. She'd much rather take it to her bedroom—wherever that was—herself. The thought of him invading the privacy of her quarters gave her a moment's unease.

Inside, the entrance hall was very large. Dell had expected it to be gloomy, but instead, it was bathed in a late-afternoon glow. Behind the large circular staircase rose an enormous mullioned window, obviously dating to more recent times than the rest of the château, but in keeping nevertheless. Some of its panels were constructed of stained glass, and faint traces of colour patched the flagstone floor of the entrance, lying in pools of muted purple and rose.

'How beautiful!' exclaimed Dell, catching her breath at the sight.

Ernestine smiled with proprietorial pride, and led her across the hall, chattering like a magpie and offering bits of information about the château. The staircase, like everything else, was massive, its stone steps worn low in the centre from the tread of many generations. Halfway up, Dell paused. Through the tall window she could see an inner courtyard and a serene garden that would be truly charming when the weather warmed. For the moment, straw still covered the rosebushes to protect against the possibility of a late mountain frost.

The four inner walls of the château, overlooking this courtyard, were a surprise. Unlike the outer walls, they were well sprinkled with large sunny windows, obviously a latter-day improvement like the one she now looked through.

'I see Madame de Briand has done a lot of renovating, and very nicely too,' observed Dell. 'She must enjoy being surrounded by beautiful things.'

Ernestine skimmed a strange look in Dell's direction. 'Monsieur Rhys has told you much about Madame?'

'Er—of course, Ernestine,' stumbled Dell, not wanting to admit that he had in fact told her nothing.

Ernestine sighed. 'Well, it is true. Madame has always taken pleasure in beauty. Even now . . .'

And before Dell had time to wonder what that might mean, Ernestine had bustled on up the stairs and started along a long shadowed corridor hung with faded tapestries, their hunting scenes dimly told in tones of ivory and russet.

Halfway along the hall Ernestine opened a door and stood back. Her smile beckoned Dell into a spacious bedroom. *'Voilà.'*

Dell entered, and gasped with pleasure. A massive carved fourposter, swathed in yellow silk, dominated the room; thick gold broadloom covered the floor. Under an ornate mantel, logs crackled in the fireplace. On a dressing table, a silver bowl of fresh flowers spoke their welcome beside an ornate collection of old stick-pins jabbed into a rose velvet cushion.

'You are content?' asked Ernestine. 'You will be comfortable here?'

'Oh, Ernestine, it's beautiful! Yes, I shall be perfectly comfortable here.' Dell twirled around happily, favouring her sore ankle as she surveyed her surroundings. If it took a month, or two, or more, to go through

the notes and writings Rhys had sent to his home, at
least she would enjoy sleeping in this room.

The window overlooked the espaliered fruit trees
in the courtyard, and the last rays of sunset slanted
through its panes. Through an open door Dell could
see a tiled bathroom. A tall vase of dried flowers stood
beside a pile of thick creamy towels and what appeared
to be a sunken bath.

Then she spotted her suitcases, across the room beside a tall hand-rubbed armoire. A suggestion of a
frown marred the smoothness of her forehead. He *had*
been in here; he knew which room she would be using.
Again the question nagged at her: who *was* he?

For a moment she considered asking Ernestine the
identity of the man who had brought her to the
château. But something stopped her. She would find
out soon enough—and Ernestine would certainly think
it strange that the driver had not introduced himself
properly at the station. To admit that he had not
done so would inevitably lead to other questions, questions Dell didn't want to answer. How could she explain to Ernestine the instant antagonism of their
meeting, when she couldn't even understand it herself?

'Is there a key to the door, Ernestine?' she asked
on impulse.

'*Mais certainement, mademoiselle. Voici.*' Ernestine
jangled the large bunch of keys that hung, chatelaine-
like, from a chain around her neck. She clicked them
through her hands, almost as if she were counting her
beads; then extracting one, she handed it to Dell.

'But you have no need to lock the door! It is very
safe. 'Owever, if you prefer ...'she shrugged her
shoulders with Gallic puzzlement over the vagaries of

foreigners, and started towards the door. 'I will return, to take you to madame. 'Alf an hour? It is enough? Then, soon after, the dinner will be served.'

'Thank you, Ernestine, that will be fine.' Dell closed the door behind the housekeeper and turned the key in the lock. She let her feet describe a limping little dance over the surface of the broadloom, and hummed while she removed her clothes. Although normally a tidy person, she flung each flimsy piece of clothing into the air and let it land with a soft whisper on the thick carpeting. Things weren't looking so bad after all! It was hard to be unhappy in a room the colour of sun, with the memory of a friendly face in your mind.

The water was hot, the bath oil had a heavenly scent, and the bath seemed to soak away the traces of travel and the last vestige of soreness in her ankle. Dell lay, luxuriating in the warmth that coursed through her body, until she realised with alarm that Ernestine would be returning very soon. She stepped out of the bath and towelled herself hastily.

What to wear? She wound the champagne-coloured towel around her body and slipped barefoot into the bedroom, the tips of her pale auburn hair wisping and darkening from contact with the water. She was still rummaging through the suitcases when there was a short rap at the door. Ernestine already!

Hugging the towel about her, she hurried to the door. She turned the key in the latch and flung the door open.

It was—*him*! The dark eyes penetrated her own and then travelled beyond. They described a slow scornful arc over the broadloom where her under-things, tights, shoes, everything lay scattered in abandoned disarray; then returned to travel with insulting deliberation over the length of her body. Dell felt the blood rise unbidden to her cheeks and clutched more tightly at the towel. *Damn* being a redhead! It laid your emotions out for all the world to see.

'You!' She recovered what dignity she could by straightening herself to her full height and tilting her chin proudly in the air, in a sort of desperate attempt to pretend that her attire was quite adequate to the occasion. 'Why are you here?'

'Your small suitcase. You left it in the back seat of the car.' He held out one hand with the carry-all case she had pushed to one side earlier, with the afghan. Somehow she had forgotten it in the confusion of arrival. 'You don't think anything else would bring me to your bedroom, do you?'

The contempt in those dark lava-stone eyes seemed to make a mockery of her skimpy defences. Dell, without the spiky-heeled shoes that had added inches to her height earlier, felt very much at a disadvantage; and for the moment she was at a loss for words.

While she tried to recover her equilibrium, she stared at him stonily, refusing to lower her eyes lest she appeared flustered—let him make what he would of the transparent colour that flooded her skin. Yet, although she didn't take her eyes off his face, she could see with the edges of her vision that he looked quite different now. Taller, more urbane ... she realised it had to do with the clothing he was wearing. Gone were the rough peasant clothes he had worn this afternoon. Instead he was clad in a lounge suit of dark velvet, an indigo blue so deep it verged on black. A perfectly knotted tie and a silk shirt the colour of Sauternes completed his ensemble. Yet somehow this civilised apparel seemed no more than a veneer, not quite in keeping with the man's true nature. Something volcanic and primitive lurked, she sensed, not far from the surface. She could see it in the tense set of his shoulders, in the broad chest that pressed at the silken stuff of his shirt, in the taut line of a mouth that looked quite dangerous ...

Who *was* he anyway?

'Thank you.' She spoke coldly, allowing the words to curl slowly over her tongue. 'You may put it there,' she indicated with a grand gesture towards a spot just inside the door. She didn't dare take the suitcase herself in case the towel slipped, and the hauteur of her words helped conceal some of her inner confusion.

The man quirked a dark brow upward. 'Surely you're not afraid of losing that bit of cloth? I didn't expect such false modesty from you.'

It was in that moment that Dell knew he had read Rhys' poetry, and the damning dedication. The thought unsettled her more than she cared to admit. But surely that could not explain his hostility! Her morals were really none of the man's business—and she knew that protestations of innocence would only demean her further in his eyes. Besides, she was certain beyond a shadow of a doubt that the man was no innocent himself. So she snapped at him:

'I don't expect total strangers to comment on my modesty—false or otherwise!'

'Then you shouldn't answer the door to strangers when you're in a state of near nudity.'

'I wouldn't have answered the door at all if I'd realised who was on the other side of it. I expected Ernestine. Now please put my case down, and leave at once.'

For answer the man moved a foot or two inside the

door, and put the carry-all down on the broadloom rug. He didn't seem in any hurry to leave. Instead, he looked around the room with maddening slowness. Dell was sure he was making a mental note of the opened suitcase, its contents spilled over the floor in apparently careless fashion. He let his eyes linger on the bed for a fraction of time too long, and then looked back at the tall, straight-limbed girl who stood so tensely in the doorway. His presence, and the unhurried insolence of his movements, were a threat to Dell's composure.

'You make yourself right at home, don't you?' he drawled.

'Of course. I expect to stay for some time.'

'Perhaps you'll change your mind. Life around here is lived at a very slow pace—there's very little excitement for a girl like you.'

'How do you know what kind of a girl I am? In any case, I'm here for business, not pleasure. Now will you please *go*?'

'As you wish.' He shrugged, and moved back to the doorway. But before he left, he wheeled around and gave her one last scathing look. 'We dress for dinner.'

The words were caustic, holding a wealth of unspoken insults. Then he turned and vanished soundlessly down the hall.

Dell felt her limbs invaded by a quivering weakness that was the aftermath of tension. So he would be joining them at table tonight! *We* dress for dinner, he had said, and obviously he *was* dressed for dinner. Still shaky, she hurried back to the suitcase and pulled out a dress of dark green velvet. It seemed to have survived the trip relatively unscathed, which was more than she could say for herself at this moment.

She had bought the dress in a moment of extravagance before leaving London. Its narrow Empire bodice moulded her bosom very tightly, and the skirt fell away in folds from beneath the compressed bustline. The sleeves were long, trailing, mediaeval in cut, and edged with a soft fall of lace.

She brushed the traces of dampness from her hair and left it to hang loose over her shoulders. Carefully she applied mascara and an understatement of green eyeshadow; it wouldn't do to look sloppy when she was about to meet a woman who had been a celebrated beauty in her day. And as for *him*—why, she told herself, she didn't really care one jot what he thought of her appearance! All the same, she chose a jewel-rich shade of lipstick and traced the outline of her lips with exquisite care.

By the time the soft knock came at the door she had tucked her feet into green glove-leather slippers and gathered up her discarded clothes, putting them neatly in a corner of the bathroom for hand-washing later that evening.

Ernestine was as jovial as ever, her square honest peasant's face warming at the sight of Dell. 'Mademoiselle is so beautiful!' she glowed, clapping her gnarled fingers in a gesture of delight. 'Monsieur Raoul—'e will be, how do you say, over-bowled!'

Monsieur Raoul. So that was his name. But who *was* he?

CHAPTER TWO

THE *salon* was a large room, a soaring piece of space, huge but somehow not solid in the way of the rest of the château. Dell looked around the room appreciatively. There were some straight chairs and chests in heavy antique carved woods; some superb nineteenth century marquetry pieces, so intricately inlaid that one could only guess at their value; a deeply cushioned, inviting island of sofas and chairs surrounding the fireplace; other smaller groupings scattered elsewhere.

On the dark polished floor lay several very old Bokhara rugs, red with the depth of colour achieved only in the Orient. The carved wood panelling, against the fireplace wall, gleamed with the patina of age and the glow of wax. The other walls, which might have once been stone, were now an airy expanse of plaster, painted bone white and covered with paintings.

The paintings! Dell couldn't be sure, but might that be a Seurat ...? And a Rousseau? She longed to move closer, to go slowly around the room, to savour the colours and draw out the pleasure of discovering each treasure. But behind her Ernestine was speaking:

'Madame de Briand, she is waiting,' she reminded Dell not unkindly. 'You must go to her—by the fireplace.' Then Ernestine closed the door gently and vanished, leaving Dell in the room.

Hesitantly, Dell moved halfway across the space toward the fireplace, and stopped. Surely Ernestine was mistaken? There was no sign of anyone; perhaps Madame de Briand had not yet come downstairs.

'Come closer, my dear.' Dell heard the lightly accented words with a little start. So Madame de Briand was there, after all!

'Come to me, Delilah; you must not be nervous. I am not an ogre.' The voice gave a throaty, marvellous little laugh: a double note, very low and musical and French. Dell, who had never been particularly fond of her full name, thought it had never sounded so beautiful.

She moved silently and swiftly over the rug towards the sound of the voice, and stopped in front of the woman. Madame de Briand was seated in a large dark wing chair, facing the fireplace. Dell hesitated. The voice with its warm inflections had sounded welcoming, but perhaps that had been a figment of imagination. For here was no outstretched hand, no rising from the chair in greeting, no turning of the face to welcome a stranger. Madame de Briand sat unmoving, head slightly tilted and shadowed by the wing of the chair, slender veined hands very fragile and very still against the dark blue silk of her dress.

'Delilah? You are there?'

With a shock Dell realised the woman must be blind. It was something she would be expected to know: Rhys would have told her—if her engagement to Rhys had been anything more than a sham. She realised how little, really, she knew about Rhys and his family.

'Delilah? It is you?'

With a rush Dell moved to the wing chair and knelt beside it. She could feel a constriction of the throat and for a moment the words refused to come, so she put out her own trembling hands and placed them over the older woman's.

'Yes, Madame de Briand.' Dell spoke finally, a tremor in her voice; and the older woman raised a hand, tentatively, exploring the air between them, as though her fingertips might brush aside the blackness, like a curtain.

'I am so happy.' The sightless eyes turned towards the younger girl's voice, and Dell thought she had never seen a face more beautiful. Madame de Briand was not young; Rhys must have been a child of her later life. She was very thin, and time had taken its toll: the hair was nearly totally white, although still thick and full-bodied; the face bore a heavy tracery of lines; the skin had lost tone and taken on the weary, insidious softness of age, like an antique panne velvet.

But the bones were still there. The bones were marvellous—high cheekbones, a well-defined curve of jaw, a straight, narrow, patrician nose. And the mouth— it was warm, expressive, alive, a remarkably young mouth in the cobwebbed texture of the face. There was something familiar about it, something Dell couldn't quite define.

'I have been so anxious for you to come.' A smile played over the mouth, revealing a set of still-strong teeth. 'Welcome to Montperdu.'

Montperdu—lost mountain. A sad name. 'I'm here now. And—and I'll be staying for a while, a month or two at least.' Dell pulled a needlepoint footstool closer to the wing chair and sat down within reach.

'Of course. I had hoped that you might stay longer ... But perhaps it is too soon to ask.'

A shadow passed over the woman's face. Dell had a

small sinking feeling, a twinge of guilt for the deceit she was about to practise. She spoke hastily to cover her momentary confusion. 'I—I'll have to see how many papers there are to go through.'

Madame de Briand laughed, again that deep-throated music bubbling from some hidden spring. 'There are many, many papers. All those years—Rhys always here, always there, always in a hotel room some-where—all those years he shipped his notes home for us to store. He used to say he should have one suitcase for his clothes and one for his manuscripts! But he lived such a—a nomadic life.' She sighed.

'I'm so sorry . . .' began Dell.

'Hush. It is a sorrow we share. You perhaps even more than I. It is a long time since he lived at home.'

'He used to talk about the Auvergne—about visiting here.' That much was true.

'We were so pleased when he became engaged.' A furrow of pain creased Madame de Briand's brow. 'We thought perhaps . . .'

'I'm sure he would have settled down,' Dell lied softly.

'And now we have so much to learn about you.' The white head leaned back against the hollow of the chair and the dark eyes stared unblinkingly into their own personal night. 'Rhys told us nothing. He wrote so much, but seldom a letter. No more than half a dozen over the years.'

'He always intended to write.' A kind little decep-tion. 'Perhaps the packages he sent home were his way of communicating.'

'Yet they told us so little——' she sighed again, more heavily. 'The newspapers were not always—flattering, but at least they told us something of his life. The newspapers ... and his books.'

Dell looked down at her tightly clenched hands with fierce embarrassment. Of course Madame de Briand must be thinking about his latest book. *That* book.

'He loved you very much.' A gentle, faraway smile softened the old woman's face, as though a vision of something beautiful had flitted across the barrier of sightlessness. 'Come, my dear, do not be embarrassed. We are women of the world.'

'I ... I'm not——' Dell bit her tongue. No use to tell Madame de Briand that Rhys had been writing about any one of a dozen others, women who had changed with every city, every mood, every season. Women he had loved with tempestuous abandon—for a time. Like that last girl, the one in Massachusetts. And others, more others than Dell could remember. But she could tell none of this to Madame de Briand. It would only hurt this magnificent woman more, and she had been hurt enough.

She tilted her chin proudly and made a difficult decision. 'I'm not embarrassed.'

Madame de Briand reached a blue-veined hand up to her throat and fingered an antique cameo pendant that lay in a pale oval against the blue silk, its chiselled delicacy merely emphasising the frailty of her frame. She looked somehow pleased. 'I, too, was once young. One remembers.'

There was a short silence as Dell groped around for something appropriate to say. Finally, a return to safe territory: 'Rhys had a very great talent.'

'We are an artistic family.' Madame de Briand spoke without false modesty: a calm acceptance of the creative gifts that a generous nature had bestowed. 'It is something in the genes, perhaps. His father was Welsh, and the Welsh have poetry in their blood. And my own ancestors were men of letters, writers, visionaries. It is a proud tradition.'

'And Rhys lived up to it,' said Dell, truthfully enough.

'Now, tell me about yourself. Everything, I must know everything.' Madame de Briand leaned forward eagerly.

Dell bit her lip. 'There's not much——'

The door opened and she looked up, thankful for the interruption. But it was a short-lived gratitude.

The man paused in the door for a fraction of time, his eyes scanning the scene, lazy-lidded, mocking. Then he strode over to the fireplace. Raoul, Ernestine had called him. Dell tried the name on in her mind and it seemed to fit. Hadn't she once read that the name was derived from a word meaning wolf? Certainly there was something animalistic about him—something lean, hungry, almost vicious. But who was he?

His next words answered her question as he leaned over the frail white-haired woman with an almost protective gentleness, as if intervening between her and Dell. 'Maman, you must not let Miss—Everett—tire you.'

Her son! Rhys' brother! But Rhys had no brother. Then she remembered. Mention had been made of another child, a son abandoned when Madame de Briand had left her husband.

'But she is not tiring me! Raoul, you forget your manners,' the old woman scolded him with affectionate ease. 'And surely you should not call your brother's fiancée *Miss* Everett. Did you not introduce yourselves properly in the long drive from the village? She will think you rude. You must call her Delilah.'

Raoul straightened and his eyes narrowed dangerously for a moment. Then, without looking at Dell, he spoke. '*Eh bien*, Delilah it is.'

The sound of her name on his tongue rankled. 'Most people call me Dell.' She couldn't keep the edge of annoyance from her voice.

'Dell! Of course. Very pretty.' On Madame de Briand's tongue, the name had a lilting cadence.

'I think Delilah is more suited.' Raoul's voice held a silky insult. He pulled a pack of cigarettes from his pocket and extracted a Gitane.

'Raoul, do stop being so stuffy and get us a sherry. Of course it shall be Dell—if you wish, my dear. You will have a sherry too?'

'Thank you.' Dell could feel the muscles of her face ache with an unreasonable resentment. How she would love to smack her hand across his disapproving face! Lucky for him Madame de Briand was present.

The sherry swirled, catching pale amber glints in the cut glass of the heavy goblets. Dell took a healthy gulp to steady her nerves, and caught his eyes slanting at her scornfully.

Madame de Briand spoke, breaking the tension between them. There was a soothing quality in her voice, almost as though she sensed the antagonism that hung in the air. 'We have so much to learn, Raoul, have we not? Dell, do tell us about yourself.'

'There's very little to tell,' Dell demurred uncomfortably, shifting on the little footstool and wishing now she had chosen to sit in one of the large chairs.

Her position put her at a decided disadvantage.

'We know you work for the publishing house of your uncle, that is all. That you—you were a sort of agent for writers, including Rhys; that this is how you met him. But about you—nothing.'

'We know some things,' murmured Raoul with infuriating calmness, but Dell chose to ignore him.

'I—I live with my aunt and uncle. My parents are dead—have been, for ten years. Their sailing boat capsized in a storm.'

'And how old are you ...? You see, my child, I cannot guess these things.' Eugénie de Briand gave a little gesture of helplessness.

'Twenty-four.'

'Twenty-four. How wonderful to be twenty-four! The world ahead of you ... But you must tell me more. I must know everything! How you look, how you walk, what you wear ...'

Just then there was a soft knock and the door opened again. It was Ernestine, come to announce that dinner had been served. Madame de Briand rose carefully and extended her hand; Raoul moved across to her and took it in his own.

The sightless face turned towards Dell. 'We do not eat in the large dining hall. It is unsuitable for small gatherings. When we are two or three, we dine in another room, litle more than an alcove really, a small but charming place.'

'It sounds wonderful. And I *am* hungry.' Dell pushed her footstool back into position and turned to follow the others.

'*C'est bien*. Unlike others in this part of the world, we eat our big meal late in the day—a habit, no doubt,

of my days in other lands.' Madame de Briand picked
her way carefully across the carpet. Raoul walked
slowly, waiting for his mother, and his face was inscrutable. 'You will not think it rude that Raoul offers
his arm to me? You are, after all, the guest. But it is a
necessity.'

Dell laughed lightly. 'I'm a big girl now.'

'Even big girls need a strong hand, now and then.'
Madame de Briand gave an exaggerated sigh. 'In my
day ...'

But the sentence was never finished and a moment
later they found themselves in the dining area. If
Madame de Briand had called this an alcove, what
would the main dining room be like? Two of her
uncle's dining room could have nested in this place,
with space to spare. On the walls were more paintings,
and a superb tapestry, very large and fine, but unlike
those upstairs this was contemporary in conception,
and intricately woven in a gorgeous sweep of mixed
colours. Once again Dell found herself wishing she
could linger over the room, touching, admiring.

The chairs were smoky with age, with tall carved
backs and ornate arms. They were polished to a fault;
Ernestine must be a splendid housekeeper. Surprisingly
they were not uncomfortable, and Dell's hands curved
appreciatively over the rubbed wood of the armrests.

A maid appeared, bearing a large fragrant bowl of
a thin clear soup. Héloise was her name, Dell dis-
covered. She was a girl from the village of Saint-Just-
sur-Haute, very young, but well trained under the
sharp eye and tongue of Ernestine.

The conversation was desultory as course followed
course: a salad made with tender green lentils and

flavoured with minced chervil; trout, subtly seasoned; a *gigot* of lamb and some potatoes of heavenly flavour —*rapée auvergnate*, Dell was told. Dessert was fresh raspberries, sweet and satisfying.

Raoul was uncommunicative throughout the meal. He seemed determined to ignore her, and that suited Dell perfectly. In any case it was surprisingly easy to converse with Madame de Briand, and Dell kept her head determinedly averted from the end of the table where those dark, insolent eyes lay in ambush, like a trap waiting to be sprung for the unwary. Madame de Briand conversed knowedgeably about a vast variety of subjects and seemed not to notice Raoul's silence.

'But, my dear! Here we are, talking about us, about the château, about the art! When it is *you* we must talk about.' Madame de Briand reached a finger very slowly to seek the saucer of her coffee cup. She managed at table with the careful expertise of practice. 'Raoul, a brandy for Dell. No? A liqueur, then? We have a very fine one in this district, not unlike Chartreuse: — the Verveine du Velay. But you must choose. Raoul, a Grand Marnier for me, please.'

Dell decided to try the paler version of the local liqueur and found it pleasant enough, but a little sweetish for her taste. For some inexplicable reason she found herself blaming Raoul, almost as though he had chosen it for her. She wished that, like him, she had taken a marc brandy after all.

'So—we talk about you.' Madame de Briand inclined her head in Dell's direction. 'You must excuse the curiosity of an old woman. It is difficult, when one cannot see.'

'What would you like to know?' Dell managed an

embarrassed laugh, hoping the enquiry would not become too personal.

'Tell me what you look like,' said Madame de Briand, leaning forward eagerly.

'I'm wearing a green dress.'

'More—tell me more.'

'I'm tall and have red hair.'

'Pah!' Madame de Briand gestured impatiently. 'I had a scrubwoman in Paris once, who could have answered that description. You are too modest about yourself. The girl will never make a writer, will she, Raoul?'

'Well, I'm quite thin,' furthered Dell.

'But you do not have a thin voice. And you do not have a scrubwoman's voice. I must know more, but I see you are unwilling to talk about yourself and will not tell me.' She turned towards the end of the table where Raoul sat, her sightless eyes pleading for his help. 'Raoul, I must depend on you. You must be my eyes. Describe her to me.'

'I'm sure she's capable of doing that herself. If she *tries*.' Raoul's voice was guarded, but his mouth was emphatically disapproving.

'Patently, she is not capable. Tell me, Raoul, what colour is her hair? Not just *red*, surely?'

Raoul's gaze travelled towards Dell with insulting slowness and trickled over her face. He let his head slope backward and rest against the high smoky wood of his chair. Dell moved uncomfortably under the penetrating, heavy-lidded appraisal. Unaccountably a look of sardonic amusement feathered over his face and transformed his scowl into a thin, derisive smile.

'The hair? Ah yes.' His voice was smooth, with a hint

of mockery. 'Titian, pure Titian. Not dyed—a pale fire. And long; it skims the shoulderblades. Too heavy to curl much, but it would if it were cut. I'd use more than a touch of gold on the little tendrils, around the ears.'

Dell sat rigidly, staring straight ahead and hoping the ready colour would not rise to her cheeks. She gripped the arms of her chair until the knuckles whitened.

'Skin very transparent, very smooth, a chamois look about it. She blushes very easily.' Dell schooled herself desperately to keep his words from coming true, and thought she had never felt such hatred for another person.

Madame de Briand smiled indulgently. 'So far, it suits the voice. You see, Dell, there are advantages to having an artist for a son. Go on, Raoul.'

So he was an artist! A dilettante dabbler, no doubt. Nevertheless this was going to be more difficult than she had thought. The man would be observant.

'The eyes are grey, a rather light grey. They shouldn't be, you know, not with that colouring. Very unusual. A London-fog look, and widely spaced. It's very deceptive, gives her a virginal appearance.'

Deceptive! Dell's fingernails dug into the wood of the armrests.

'Nose, quite unremarkable.' Dell wished she could wring his neck.

'And the mouth, Raoul?' urged Madame de Briand.

'Much too wide. Too—generous. I'd wipe that lipstick off if I was going to paint her. It makes her look——'

'Cheap?' Dell thrust in, with barely restrained annoyance.

'You said it, not I.' His voice held more than a trace of derisiveness. He was enjoying her discomfiture.

'Oh, Raoul, you are too silly!' Madame de Briand interjected, with a cluck of her tongue. 'A woman must have her little bit of artifice. Armour against the world, n'est-ce pas? Now—more. The chin, please. I am beginning to see her.'

'The chin? Right now, very indignant. Tilted fiercely. But there's a little pulse working there; the chin would like to tremble if it were allowed. Rather an interesting chin, all things considered. The bone structure is quite adequate, high cheekbones, good planes. It should be painted in an early morning light.'

Not by you, Dell thought murderously.

Eugénie de Briand leaned forward impatiently. 'Go on, Raoul! Don't stop at the chin. The rest—tell me about the rest.'

'The rest of me is really not worth talking about,' said Dell with a touch of desperation. 'Please, Madame de Briand ...'

'Oh, my dear, you must forgive me.' The older woman brushed her eyes in an apologetic gesture. 'We will stop if you prefer.' A shadow of disappointment passed across her face.

Dell hesitated. 'N-no, it's all right. I just feel rather like—like a butterfly, pinned to a wall. But please, do go ahead.'

'A Monarch butterfly, I would guess!' laughed Madame de Briand, relaxing once more. 'With your permission, then ... Raoul.' She nodded towards her son.

'Ah yes, the rest.' Raoul looked thoughtfully at Dell and tapped a cigarette against the table. He paused for a moment to light it and inhale. Then he leaned back and continued his meticulous surveillance. 'She is tall, too tall for my taste.'

Isn't that just too bad! Dell turned to stare at him mulishly and realised it was the first time she had done so all evening. Well, she wouldn't give him the satisfaction of avoiding his gaze any longer.

'Too thin to be a true Titian model; from the neck down she is more Modigliani. She moves rather well. A little too—what is the word? Provocative, perhaps.'

Dell forced herself to smile coldly at him. She'd show him who was provocative! The man really must dislike her; but why? He was not his brother's keeper.

'The hands ... let me see. Well kept. Healthy nails, cut recently. Lonk slender fingers, but not tapered enough to be truly artistic and not square enough to be totally practical. The hands betray the emotions. The chin and the mouth may be well schooled, but the hands are not.'

Dell snatched the offending members from the tablecloth, where they had been poking fiercely at a scattering of stray crumbs.

'Her dress is very—artful. Dark green velvet. I'd mix it with a trace of Prussian blue. A Catherine de Medici look about it. Very soft and ... secretive. Mediaeval sleeve with a trailing of lace, very clever that, a touch of innocence.'

Dell restrained the desire to stick out her tongue at him, like a naughty schoolgirl. To hell with him!

'The neckline is cut low and square, rather less innocent than the sleeve ... a white column of neck, no jewellery.' Surely the catalogue must be coming to an end! 'The waistline is high, with the skirt falling in soft folds, very feminine.' Madame de Briand gave a small satisfied smile, and Raoul continued. 'A bosom out of a Hans Holbein painting. Much too small.'

Now the blush came, a stain of fury that swept across her face and shot sparks of anger into her eyes.

'Oh, and she has a temper.' His voice was deceptively light. As if to give it the lie he ground his cigarette into the ashtray with cool, thorough contempt.

'Wonderful!' Madame de Briand clapped her hands delightedly. 'A daughter-in-law after my own heart!'

'Not quite a daughter-in-law,' said Raoul, his voice suddenly very quiet and lethal.

'Raoul!' Madame de Briand was clearly more than a little annoyed. She turned to Dell placatingly. 'Forgive Raoul; he has the manners of a peasant. To me, it is as if you were my daughter-in-law.'

Dell slanted a chilling glance towards the offending man and articulated the words carefully. 'Thank you. I consider it an honour.'

'You see, Raoul? She has spirit, too. Dell, to me you will be a member of the family. Ignore Raoul. He will be rude when it pleases him, but he is brutally honest; he cannot lie even to himself. He has painted me a picture of you and I like the picture. You must call me Eugénie.' The woman was clearly pleased.

'I shall be delighted ... Eugénie.'

CHAPTER THREE

THE morning light quivered behind the curtains. Dell stirred luxuriantly and pulled the silken sheet over her head, burrowing her face into the pillow. But it was too fine to lie for long, and within moments she slipped out of the massive bed—one felt very small in a bed this size—and into her dressing gown, a smoky pink velour. She had slept naked as always, and the fabric felt good, soft and warm as a new kitten.

It had rained in the night, but now the sunlight lay over the courtyard like a thin golden syrup. The day was going to be beautiful. It would be a splendid day for exploring, for putting on a pair of stout walking shoes and tramping over the greening hills in search of what the countryside had to offer. But one had to face the fact that this was a working holiday.

It was still very early and Dell wondered if the household would be awake. As if in answer to her question, a man emerged into the courtyard. He was short and heavy-set, with pouched eyes, and he was clad in rough working clothes. He carried a trowel, plus assorted gardening equipment, under his good arm; the other was bound in a makeshift sling of some kind. With his good hand he started to pull the straw away from the rose bushes and move it into neat piles, ready for removal. Summer was coming to the courtyard.

Dell showered swiftly in the modern bathroom. Then she moved to the armoire to select an outfit for the day. She settled on a forest-green corduroy skirt and patterned blouse. A large cheval mirror stood near the armoire and as she slipped out of her bathrobe, she remembered Raoul's remark with an excess of annoyance. Bosom too small, was it! Released from the confines of the tight bodice her contours were hardly flat. Perhaps the velvet dress had been a poor choice after all.

Decisively she replaced the printed blouse on a hanger and took out a tight turtleneck of fine wool the colour of new butter. She flipped the bra back in a drawer; she'd show him! The skinny turtleneck clung brazenly to her figure, hugging the rise of her breast and defining the curves with precise clarity. It left very little to the imagination.

Downstairs Héloise was polishing the brasses of the large front door, attacking them with a ferocity that left no doubt in Dell's mind as to where the gleam of the château came from. The girl looked up at Dell with a shy smile and put down her polishing rag. She bobbed her head and murmured an apology in French, indicating that Dell should enter the dining alcove where they had eaten last night. But Dell shook her head. She had no desire to disturb the day's schedule.

'*Je vais manger plus tard*,' she enunciated carefully, '*avec* Madame.'

Just then Ernestine bustled out, fresh apron flying, and Dell was glad she did not have to strain her limited knowledge of French further.

'Madame does not descend until late in the day,' explained Ernestine. 'Breakfast for you, it is no trouble! Monsieur Raoul, he eats breakfast when it pleases him. He has eaten an hour ago, this morning.'

'Perhaps—could I just eat in the kitchen, Ernestine? I'd love to see it.'

'The kitchen?' Ernestine looked shocked. 'Of course I will take you to see the kitchen. But you must eat in the dining room.' This very firmly; Ernestine would brook no nonsense of a mere visitor interfering with the order of things.

The kitchen was huge, very clean, and hung with interesting old pots and pans in burnished copper. There was an enormous fireplace, large enough to roast an ox, and Dell was certain that in days gone by it had been used for just that. A long, spotless wooden table stood squarely in the centre of the room, and along the length of one wall gleamed a row of modern appliances. At the large copper-hooded stove stood an ample woman clad in worn, comfortable slippers and a shapeless skirt. Her apron, like Ernestine's, was spotless. The woman eyed Dell suspiciously and Dell noticed a faint growth of hair above the short upper lip.

'This is Marie-Ange, Mademoiselle Everett.' Dell smiled generously and the woman acknowledged it with an economical bob of her head. 'Marie-Ange is very jealous of her kitchen. But she cooks like an angel.'

'Tell her not to be afraid, I'm a rotten cook,' laughed Dell. 'I won't be interfering.' Ernestine murmured a few words to the woman and Marie-Ange's strong teeth broke into a wide, uneven smile, her homely face radiating its own particular brand of beauty.

'Even *I* do not dare touch in the kitchen!' remarked Ernestine as she led Dell back to the dining alcove. 'That is the *ressort*—the—the province of Marie-Ange.'

'And who is the man I saw working in the garden this morning?' Dell sat down at the table and shook a crisply ironed linen napkin over her knees.

'Ah, that is Gaspard, the chauffeur and gardener. But Monsieur Raoul will have told you yesterday ...' Ernestine helped Dell to a generous serving of sweetbreads and scrambled eggs. 'Gaspard has an accident, just as he is leaving to pick you up at the station. But it is a little sprain only, not so serious as we had suspected. Monsieur Raoul, he is not so happy to drive the old car, but his own is not good for carrying the luggage. You will 'ave some bacon?'

Dell declined, and picked up her knife and fork. So that was why Raoul had come for her, instead of the chauffeur!

'Ernestine, there are papers here that Monsieur Rhys has sent over the years.' Ernestine nodded knowingly, just the trace of a well-hidden gleam escaping her eye. So she had read Rhys' book too ... probably out loud, to Madame de Briand. Dell attacked the scrambled eggs.

'I'd like to see them after breakfast. Can you show me where they are?'

'*Non, mademoiselle*, I am sorry.' She shook her head emphatically. 'Only Monsieur Raoul, 'e keeps the key to that room.' She touched a finger to the chain that hung around her neck, and the keys jangled faintly. 'I 'ave no key.'

'I see. And where will I find Monsieur Raoul?' Dell sipped at the stingingly hot coffee. It was perfectly delicious.

'I do not know when will be his return. He is gone in the car, early this morning.'

Dell felt a stab of irritation, a sensation that was becoming altogether too familiar. Raoul knew perfectly well that she had come to see Rhys' papers. He might at least have left the key for her.

'Well, thank you, Ernestine.' Perversely, she felt disappointed now, although earlier she had wanted to explore the local terrain and forget the day's work.

Might as well change into the walking shoes after all, she decided. It was a fine day and it was no use sitting inside, waiting for someone who mightn't turn up until nightfall.

Outside, the air was rinsed by rain, and the sun was considerably warmer than yesterday. Even Montperdu looked less grisly today. Dell felt her spirits soar as she picked her way cautiously over the cobbled stones of the courtyard. No more twisted ankles today, thank you!

The gravel of the road was still dark and damp from rain. Treacherous puddles lay in hollows, their skin glistening in the sun like pools of quicksilver. Small rivulets trickled their way lazily down the slope of the road, and somewhere a curious liquid note trilled, an oriole perhaps, sounding distant and faintly foreign.

Halfway down the single-lane mountain pass there was an enormous outcropping of rock. For some distance the road had been blasted through, leaving bleak walls of lava rock on either side. They rose high and steep, small tufts of broom catching a precarious hold here and there.

The road was very narrow at this point. A bed of gravel had been laid many years before, and presumably it had once provided a level surface. But years of torrential rainstorms had washed away much of the gravel in the centre, channelling the run-off into tyre ruts, carving the depressions ever more deeply until now the road bed was shaped rather like a giant U. The single lane allowed ample room for a car to pass through, but the steep banking of the sides was such that a person on foot could only walk along the rutted depression of the centre. It gave Dell the sensation of walking through a long tunnel. It was gloomy here, and cooler than in the sun. Dell shivered.

From the distance, she could hear the sounds of a car approaching. There was a shifting of gears, a swift scrunch of tyres storming the surface of the gravel. It seemed to be drawing near very swiftly and Dell quickened her pace. With luck, she could pass this cut in the road before the car arrived. She looked at the walls of rock with growing apprehension. There seemed nowhere to go. The rise of land on either side of the tyre ruts was far too steep for her feet to find purchase. And it was impossible to see where the rock cut ended; the road twisted so much it obscured her vision.

She started to run, but the gravel caught at her feet and the pain in her ankle flared again. Damn! The car was nearly here, possibly around the next bend ...

As the car appeared, she did the only thing she could do: she hurled herself at one of the steeply banked walls and reached for a clump of broom, trying desperately to pull her feet out of the depression where the tyres would travel. The car whizzed by, brakes screeching, with inches to spare, and the clump of broom pulled away from the wall, dragging a shower of thin soil after its shallow roots.

Not a moment too soon. Dell lay sprawled in the road, her heart palpitating fiercely and her skirt contorted about her knees in an ungainly fashion. The car had ground to a halt farther along the road, and she looked at it dazedly, half expecting to see the battered Renault. But it was a sleek sports model, low-slung and gleaming in a dark sable brown. Even before she saw him she knew the driver would be Raoul.

He came down the road like an avenging angel, a dark thunderhead of a man.

'You crazy fool! You could have killed yourself!' His eyes blazed with anger and he stood above her, arms akimbo. Not even a gesture to help her to her feet.

'Who's calling who crazy? You were driving like a madman.' Dell brushed the gravel from her knees. Her pantyhose were ripped, badly, and a few grains of stone had caught uncomfortably beneath the sheer nylon. 'Anyway, there was nowhere for me to go.'

'You might try using your eyes.' He waved his hand angrily at the far side of the road, and for the first time Dell noticed a depression in the wall of rock, a small hollow half hidden by a scrubby overgrowth of vegetation. 'There are several of those walk-ins, spaced along the road. You're supposed to get into one when you hear a car coming.'

Dell pulled herself shakily to her feet and surveyed the damage. Fortunately her coat had survived; it was the only one she had brought with her to France. But one shoe had been torn off in the struggle to escape the car's onslaught, and it lay demolished on the road, a flattened caricature of a brogue. She picked it up and grimaced. 'Is that all you can say?' she demanded.

'This might have been me, you know.' She shook the shoe in his face.

'Hardly a great loss,' he said with biting sarcasm. 'Nevertheless, I'm glad it's not. Come on, I'll take you back to the château. You seem to have a penchant for twisted ankles.' So he had noticed, yesterday!

He put out an arm and gripped her elbow firmly. Dell jerked it away as if scorched, and started to hobble towards the car. It was very hard to look dignified with one shoe off.

Raoul laughed. Dell felt her hackles rise and stifled the urge to kill. He had the audacity to laugh at her, when he was responsible for her plight! There was a slow burning sensation in the pit of her stomach, a turmoil of hatred for this man with his supercilious ways and his wretched manners. Somehow he always managed to put her in the wrong.

He caught up to her easily, and passed by, reaching the car long before she did. But this time he didn't bother to hold the door open for her. Instead he jack-knifed his long limbs into the driver's seat and waited coolly while Dell struggled with the door on her side.

The car switched into a throaty purr before she had even settled in her seat, and she slammed her door viciously in revenge. He jammed the gear into first and let out the clutch, jerking forward so that she was thrown breathlessly against the back of the seat.

'Quite the dominant male, aren't you?' she gave voice to her pique. 'Always right about everything.'

'That's right,' he concurred coolly. The car negotiated a hairpin curve without a flicker of change in speed. 'For once I am in total agreement with you.'

Dell gritted her teeth and tried to turn her attention to the car—a Turbo Porsche, she had noted as she entered, with bucket seats so moulded that they might have been poured to fit her body. But she remained totally, annoyingly conscious of him. His hands on the wheel were disturbingly competent—strong tapered fingers, a light dusting of hair creeping out from the sleeve of his heavy cable-knit sweater. He was wearing a white sweater today, and it made him look almost swarthy, the hollows and planes of his face more pronounced than ever. The muscles of his legs stretched tautly beneath the brown suede trousers, tensing and relaxing as he changed gear, braked and accelerated with the smoothness of total assurance. She might have been shaken by the encounter at the pass, but he certainly had not. She longed for a way to prick his complacency: this self-important chauvinist with his over-inflated ego.

In the courtyard of the château, Gaspard was at work on the ancient Renault, his good hand tinkering greasily with something under the raised bonnet.

Raoul braked the Porsche to a halt and slid out without another word to Dell. He extracted a small parcel of wire from the floor of the car and strolled lazily over to the other man.

He can't get rid of me that easily! fumed Dell, stepping out of the car and hopping on one foot over to the Renault. Her inoperative shoe dangled dispiritedly from one hand.

Gaspard straightened and doffed his hat, a much-worn leather cap with earlugs. Dell smiled; Gaspard smiled unsurely, glancing at Raoul for direction. When none was forthcoming he returned uncertainly to his work. Raoul pointedly ignored her.

'You might introduce me.' Dell gritted the words out through clenched teeth.

'Gaspard, meet Delilah.' The implied insult was perfectly intentional. Gaspard looked up again and smiled nervously; he at least had the grace to look embarrassed.

'Mademoiselle Everett,' he acknowledged, and Dell smiled at him before turning back to Raoul.

'I need to get at those papers,' Dell said abruptly.

Raoul continued to run his fingers skilfully over a tangle of electrical connections. 'Oh?'

'I need the key now.'

He straightened wearily and looked her in the eye. 'You didn't need it so badly half an hour ago. You were aiming off for a morning's hike.'

'Nevertheless.' She stood her ground.

He clicked his tongue in annoyance. 'All right, Gaspard, do what you can without me,' he said in French. 'I'll be right back.'

In the front hall, Ernestine clucked sympathetically as she took Dell's coat, surveying the wreckage of pantyhose and shoes with alarm. I really am a mess, thought Dell, looking down at the ruined pantyhose in dismay, and wishing she hadn't made an issue of getting the key from Raoul right now. She should be back in her room, washing off the dust and the remnants of gravel, and finding herself some fresh clothes.

But Raoul was standing there, waiting with exaggerated patience by the door to the study. Dell sat down to remove her remaining shoe. Then, barefoot, she padded into the study behind him.

Raoul closed the door decisively and moved over to the large antique desk that stood to one side of the room. Bookshelves honeycombed the walls, reaching solidly to the ceiling, and a bookladder leaned negligently against one shelf on wheeled feet. A small pile of books, obviously in use, lay in casual disorder on the edge of the carpet near the ladder. The carpet itself was a Kerman, rather old and quite worn. Leather armchairs were grouped against the far wall, around a contemporary table of heavy polished plate glass.

Dell remained standing while Raoul rummaged through the drawers of the desk. Finally he extracted a small envelope and shook two keys out of it. One he replaced in the drawer, the other he kept in his hand. Then he rose and moved around the desk towards her.

She held out her hand, but he made no move to give her the key. Instead, he tossed it lightly into the air and retrieved it with a supple flip of his wrist.

'Don't you think you'd better do something about your appearance first?' The fact that the thought coincided so exactly with Dell's own earlier assessment merely annoyed her.

'I'll change when I'm good and ready,' she said flatly. 'May I have the key?'

'You have trouble with words like please, don't you?' He smiled down at her thinly, and pocketed the key. 'In any case, first things first. You need a bath. You're a mess.'

'You already made my defects quite clear, last night.'

'Did I? Well, I see I was mistaken about one of them.' His eyes slid downward and fastened on the rise of breast beneath her pale sweater. Damn, thought Dell, whatever possessed me this morning ... Something rare and strange shivered along the nerve pathways of her body, and she could feel the traitorous nipples visibly hardening beneath his gaze. It was as though he had reached out his hand to touch her. She wheeled angrily towards the door. No man had ever dared to look at her in quite that fashion before. She felt suddenly bitter and defeated.

'If you give me the key now I won't have to bother you for it later,' she said tonelessly.

'Come back in half an hour.' The rejoinder was gruff. 'I'll be finished with Gaspard shortly, then I'll take you to the room myself.'

Twenty minutes later Dell had showered herself back to respectability. She changed into a pair of blue denim jeans and a long-sleeved cotton shirt, finely checked in red and white. Her hair, still damp from the shower, was caught up pony-fashion in a length of red velvet ribbon. Hardly the femme fatale now.

As she expected, she found Raoul in the courtyard, still working with Gaspard on the mechanical problems of the car. He too had changed, into a pair of pale blue cords that bore traces of oil paints, as well as smudges of grease from the engine. The heavy white cabled sweater was gone and in its place was a close-fitting navy blue turtleneck, accentuating the muscular set of his shoulders.

He straightened at her approach and spoke a few low words to Gaspard in French. Then he wiped his fingers over the stained pockets of his trousers and looked at Dell critically, hands on hips.

'An improvement, I'd say.' A ghost of a smile loomed over his lips, but there was no humour in it.

'I can't say the same for you,' returned Dell, irritably, eyeing his work clothes.

'Some people have more room for improvement

than others.' There was a deliberate, measured rude-
ness to the words, and as if to emphasise his annoyance, he ran his fingers impatiently through his hair.
'Shall we get this over with?'

Dell snapped him a look that was intended to be
devastating, and came full tilt against the sardonic
coolness of his gaze. The man was impossible! Were
there no chinks in his armour?

Perhaps it was time for a change of tactics.

CHAPTER FOUR

THE room where Rhys' papers were stored took its shape from the turret in which it was located. A bulbous, dark room, it still emanated a mediaeval chill which was not noticeable in other parts of the château. The walls were stone, the furnishings sparse, and the room had a little-used dankness about it.

In the centre of the room was a large, baronial dark oak table. What little light filtered in through the high slits of window seemed to be dissipated by the time it reached room level. Cardboard cartons and fat brown-paper envelopes were stacked idly against one barren wall, most still tied and postmarked. Dell shivered. Not the most congenial surroundings for the work she had to do!

She hesitated at the threshold, taking her bearings in the dim light, while Raoul walked across the room and switched on a large dim desk light. It did little more than serve as an exclamation point to emphasise the shadowed surroundings. The circle of light it cast on the oaken table picked out a small pile of letters, envelopes bearing the postage stamps of half a dozen countries. A fine powdering of dust lay over the surface of the table.

Raoul turned and half-sat on the rim of the desk, arms folded. A frown cut his brow deeply as he surveyed the scene.

'You'll need more light in here.'

Dell managed a half smile. 'Yes, another lamp would help.' It was going to be uphill work, stifling her resentment towards this irritating man. Then, as an afterthought: 'Please.'

'Done,' he said easily.

Dell watched with a kind of prickling fascination as Raoul's free leg swung rhythmically in and out of the shadows cast by the single light. He seemed in no hurry to go.

'Would you have a typewriter I could use? I could put it ... here.' She walked over and pulled a small table closer to the large desk.

'We'll get one.' He looked at her, unsmiling and speculative.

Dell swallowed the irritation that always seemed to rise in her, unaccountably, at his simplest remarks. She looked at him, a sidelong look, and smiled sweetly. 'It's very good of you.'

His eyes remained fathomless. 'Anything else?' He was still curt; it would take some work yet.

'Paper. Lots of paper. Pencils, pens, that sort of thing. And if you wouldn't mind——' she paused. There was a soft parting of her lips as she touched her tongue to them.

'Yes?'

'—The key to the room.' A velvet lowering of the lashes.

In answer, he reached into his pocket and brought out the key. Dell put her hand forward to take it, but he held it just out of her reach. A sardonic smile edged his mouth, briefly.

'I preferred you the other way.'

She looked at him, speechless for a moment, and she

felt the hot anger flooding up from the depths of her being. 'What do you mean!'

How dared he see through her!

'As a spitfire, you're honest. As a flirt . . .' he shrugged his shoulder nonchalantly, and flung the key on to the dusty table, '. . . you're a failure.'

Dell stamped her foot on the floor in a fury of frustration. 'Get out! Get out—now—before—before I——'

'See what I mean? On you, it comes naturally.' Was he laughing at her?

'I mean it. Get out!'

'I'll go when I'm finished with what I have to say to you. And not before.'

'You and I have nothing to say to each other! Just—leave me alone.'

'With your memories?' He gestured at the dusty cartons tilting dispiritedly against the far wall.

'My—memories—as you call them, are none of your business.' She flung her hair back defiantly; he was getting entirely too personal.

Suddenly his voice became silky, threatening. 'Your memories *are* my business when they interfere with the happiness of my mother.' He moved a step closer and looked down at her, his brows drawing together in a dark line. 'There are things she doesn't know.'

'What do you mean?' Dell felt her hands grow clammy. He was standing too near for comfort.

'About Rhys' suicide.' He lashed the words at her, like a whip.

She felt her heart beating a tattoo against her ribs. What was he driving at? She looked at him uncertainly, the question in her eyes. 'Suicide?'

'Don't look like that, little Miss Innocence.' His lip curled with disbelief.

'I don't know what you're talking about.' Dell felt the colour, for once, drain from her face. The whole situation seemed rather dreamlike, out of context, like a surrealistic stage setting.

'Don't you?' Deftly he plucked an envelope from the small pile of correspondence on the desk. Dell recognised Rhys' handwriting; postage stamps from the United States; a cancellation mark, read upside down, that might have been something like Miss., Mass.— Massachusetts, probably.

'His last letter.' Raoul tapped the envelope on the table, shaking out a single sheet of folded paper on hotel stationery. 'By the time this arrived, he was dead. But then it won't tell you anything you don't already know.'

Dell felt a constriction at the base of her throat. This really was unfair. She forced her gaze to meet his levelly. 'Try me.'

'Read it for yourself.' He tossed the letter on the table, and Dell resisted the impulse to snatch it up and rip it into small bits. Instead she continued to gaze at him coldly.

'No?' he continued. 'Well, I'll tell you, then, if the truth is too painful for you to face. Rhys wrote just before he—just before that final drunken binge. He told us everything. It's all there.'

God, what *had* Rhys told them? thought Dell, remembering those last painful days of Rhys' life ... the searching through bars, the going from hotel to hotel, the awful guilt of knowing her uncle counted on her to keep Rhys out of trouble, the sense of failure ...

'What did he tell you?' she asked as calmly as she could.

Raoul picked up the letter and quoted a passage at random. 'Ah, yes ... " as God is my witness she is driving me to madness" ...'

'Me?' Shock waves sounded in Dell's voice. 'Does he mention me by name?'

'He doesn't have to. It's you, all right. "My fiancée" ... he says it quite clearly.' Raoul's fist clenched over the letter, crumpling it vehemently. 'Rhys goes into all the gory details. About how you were—playing around.'

'*I* was——'

'To be blunt, you were unfaithful to him.'

'But——' Good heavens, it must have been that dark-haired Radcliffe student, the one Rhys had made such a play for. Sally, that was her name.

'Do you deny you were in Chicago with him?' Raoul interrupted her train of thought.

'No, but——'

'Do you deny you were his fiancée?'

'N-no.' A cold fear clutched at her.

'Then it's quite clear.' Raoul threw the crumpled letter down in disgust. 'Within days, Rhys was dead.'

'Look, I had nothing to do with that! I'm sorry about Rhys, but ...'

'Sorry! You're *sorry*! I'm sorry you ever came here. You, the person he loved and trusted—the person who destroyed him.'

Dell swallowed painfully with the effort of controlling the two hard, stinging fireballs that were her eyes

'If that's what you believe——'

'That's what I know. What my mother believes is something else. Only because I haven't told her—never will tell her—the truth.' His face was grim in the eerie light of the room. 'There are some things I couldn't hide from her. Ernestine reads the newspapers to her every day. The local papers were always quick to pick up any news of Rhys.' His voice was bitter. 'Local boy makes good. The scandalous love-child of the de Briand line.'

He dug his fingers into the edge of the table as if to gouge the very wood. 'And you——' he looked at her accusingly, 'you betrayed him.'

'Raoul, it wasn't me! You've got to believe me. The whole thing was a sham—our whole engagement was a sham.'

One black eyebrow raised itself. 'That, I believe.'

'That's not what I mean. It was done for Rhys, to keep him out of scrapes. Rhys was always—getting himself into trouble.'

'Death is a very final kind of trouble.' Raoul tapped a cigarette out of his pack and flicked a wooden match sharply, on one thumbnail. 'Too bad you couldn't keep him out of that.' He inhaled angrily.

'You don't understand, do you?' Oh, the impossibility of explaining! 'It's years since you've seen Rhys —you couldn't have really known him at all! He was —mixed up. He needed someone, for protection——'

'Someone like you?' His voice was a study in scorn. 'I'd as soon be protected by a rattlesnake.' He ground his cigarette, scarcely smoked, on to the stone floor.

'You—you insufferable, impossible, holier-than-thou prig! You weren't there and you don't know anything about it, and yet you blame *me* for Rhys' death.' The tears were very nearly defying her efforts at control. Her vision was swimming at the edges and she had a strong sense of unreality, as though her whole nightmarish world were centred around this dark, avenging man; this near-stranger who had turned her world topsy-turvy in a mere twenty-four hours. He was standing very close now, taut as a coiled spring, intensity in every lean hard muscle of him, accusation in every line of his face.

'Yes—I blame you for his death.' The words were clenched out in a hiss of hatred, and they loomed large, filling the sudden silence of the room.

Dell felt her insides ache with a soundless scream of denial. What would be the use of it? He had made his opinion of her perfectly clear, and he didn't look like the type of man who would easily change his mind. She half-turned from him, pressing her fingers to her eyelids in an effort to stem the threatened tide. At least she could try to salvage her self-respect.

The moment of weakness was over. There would be no tears now. She squared her shoulders and dropped her arms from her face, clenching her fists by her sides. She didn't dare turn around to face him again: self-control was shaky at best.

'You'd better go,' she intoned.

He took a long stride that brought him within inches of her hair. Dell could feel the come-and-go of his breath, the soft feathering of it over her hairline, the warm masculine scent of him; and something very like fear invaded the tiny invisible hairs of her skin.

Behind her back his hands raised and circled her throat, tangling in her hair, fingertips reaching around her slender neck. 'You killed him——'

His fingers tightened their pressure, very slowly, and Dell stood very still, scarcely daring to breathe. The lean strength of his fingers was like a velvet vice, hardening almost imperceptibly, sending messages of alarm shivering through her system. The room reeled, but whether it was with the touch of him or with the thought of what he could so easily do, she was not sure.

'You killed him,' the voice murmured into her ear, making a mockery of all her carefully constructed defences, 'as surely as if you had been driving that car yourself.'

'I didn't,' she whispered, senses spinning with the barely contained pressure of his fingers. She was totally aware of his nearness: the hard length of his body that grazed her shoulders, her spine, the back of her hair. A tingling warmth, almost a lassitude, spread its way down from the cruel caress of his hands. She wanted to resist yet she could not; she was suffused with a strange weakness. Her hands felt heavy, useless; her feet rooted themselves to the ground with an unaccustomed feeling of helplessness.

'Please . . .' she choked the word out, her voice barely audible against the thunder in her ears.

'Oh, God,' he muttered thickly, and suddenly she was free. Dell almost stumbled, as if she had been a puppet, suspended by his fingers and then all at once released. From behind a hand gripped her by the shoulder to steady her, and she leaned against it weakly. All the spirt had drained from her body, it seemed, and she was a trembling shell of herself. She raised a hand, slowly, and rubbed the hollows of her throat where his hands had so recently rested. The memory of his touch seemed to sting her skin, and the thought swirled in her head: *so this is why he hates me* ...

'You killed him,' repeated Raoul, 'and I can't forgive you for that.' Very deliberately, he took her shoulders and swivelled her body so that she faced him. The heavy table was behind her now, and he closed in ... so close, Dell could feel his tendons straining against her thighs. His hands gripped the table on either side of her now, crowding her against it, imprisoning her as surely as she had been imprisoned by his fingers only moments ago.

His face leaned over hers, and it was very dark and near and unforgiving. She was supremely conscious of the strength and the length of him, of the broad shoulders looming over her, of the way his eyes had gone near-black in the uncertain light. She could feel her breath coming raggedly, tearing at her lungs; her heart hammering against her ribs ... or was it his heart?

'Please!' Again the word escaped her lips, a breathless little prayer of a word, but like a cruel fate he chose not to hear it.

'Nothing—nothing you ever do or say will let my mother know the truth of your relationship with Rhys.'

'I don't know what you mean,' she whispered, staring at him as if transfixed. Was this fear shivering through her veins ... or was it something else?

'Don't you?' The words grated at her. 'I think you do. If you tell my mother that Rhys committed suicide, I won't be responsible for my actions. She is an old woman and she has had enough pain in her life, without you.'

'I wouldn't tell her that.' Dell's lashes fell in a flutter of panic. 'It's not true. His death was an accident, a terrible accident.'

'Lie to my mother, but don't lie to me! I know how you treated Rhys. I know what kind of a woman you are. The evidence is all there. Rhys' letter, his poetry——'

Dell squeezed her eyes tightly against the horror of what was happening. How could she deny, now, that Rhys had been writing about her, when she had tacitly admitted it, last night, by her silence?

Raoul's hand travelled upward and found the little pulse that beat wildly beside her ear. His voice was a low torture: 'Is it guilt that makes your heart race so, I wonder? Or do you have enough conscience to feel guilt in that pretty little head of yours?' For a moment his thumb dug in, bruising the skin. Then he reached back and made a fist in her hair, pulling her head backward until her face tilted up to his own.

'Open your eyes,' he rasped. When Dell failed to obey, he repeated: 'I said open your eyes. Look at me.' His hand jerked a command into the entwined tangle of her hair, and Dell's eyes shot open. She trembled; his face was so close that its breath might have been her own.

'That's better.' A switchblade smile flicked across the harsh planes of his face, without softening it. Dell noticed, irrelevantly, that there were tiny pale flecks, like gold, in the midnight of his eyes. Her limbs ached with the pressure of his thighs against hers. Oh God, would he never leave her alone!

'Now listen to me.' There was a rough edge to his voice; it seemed to burn into her consciousness. 'You'll work on Rhys' papers only in this room. Nothing—I repeat nothing—is to leave here until I've seen it personally.'

'But—in her letter your mother said ...'

'I know what she said,' he cut in abruptly. 'The letter be damned! I won't have anything coming out of here that could hurt my mother—that Ernestine could report to her.'

'But she already knows that—that Rhys was no angel.'

'His last book made that quite clear.' Raoul's eyes scorched her, dropping from her lashes to the quivering curve of her lips and lingering there. Dell felt the look almost like a palpable sensation, as though his own lips had seized her, bruised her. She caught her lower lip between her teeth in an effort to control its trembling. Against her scalp she could feel his thumb, moving slowly, hurtfully, as if of its own accord.

'It's true Rhys was no angel,' Raoul's voice went on, inexorably. 'She doesn't care about that—she's known that for years. But she doesn't know that his death was a suicide.'

'It wasn't!' Now there was more than a hint of desperation in Dell's denial. Was there nothing she could say to convince him?

'Oh?' A cold twist of the mouth tugged at the muscles of his jaw. 'Read the letter.'

For a moment longer he hovered over her, drawn as though he had a need to say more—but then, suddenly, his hand jerked free of her hair. With a muffled curse he thrust himself away from her. Dell, released at last, clung to the solid reassuring surface of the table, her emotions collapsing about her. She felt limp, like a rag doll that had lost its stuffing.

And the way Raoul was looking at her did nothing to restore her sense of balance. For an awful, earth-shaking instant his eyes held her as though they could see into her very soul. *But if you can see into my soul, Raoul de Briand, devil incarnate, why can't you see the truth that is there?*

Without another word he turned on his heel and stalked towards the door. Then he was gone.

Dell sank to her knees beside the table, all the fight gone from her body. The cold flagstone of the floor cut into her flesh, but she felt nothing. Only a terrible numbness.

CHAPTER FIVE

Time seemed to have lost its importance. Was it half an hour, an hour—or just five minutes since Raoul had left? Dell felt the beginnings of strength trickle back to her bones. But the shattering experiences of the morning had left her with a curious lightheadedness, an unpleasant dizzy distortion of the senses. Or was it just the strange play of light and shadow, the faint smell of mildew that hung over the room?

Then she realised it was hunger. All that emotion and then to be hungry! I guess I really am resilient after all, she thought to herself with a rueful grimace, pulling herself shakily to her feet.

Some time during that dreadful scene with Raoul, part of her shirt had tugged itself loose from the waist of her jeans, and she smoothed it back in place with unsteady fingers. Strange, even her skin felt different, more alive somehow, as if every little nerve and blood vessel had been shaken awake after the jangling nightmare of the encounter.

Well, it was over now and she was still in one piece. Her hands explored the contours of her throat tentatively: a little sore, but it would be all right. Curious how danger-prone she seemed to have become in the past day—first the ankle; then the terror of that moment on the road; now this.

And through it all, like a satanic theme, loomed that dark and vengeful face of Raoul de Briand. Dell shuddered. At least, now, she knew why he hated her. He blamed her for the death of his half-brother.

Read the letter, Raoul had said. It lay, crumpled, on the dusty desk, and she reached for it with a dread of what it might say.

The letter, it seemed, had been written shortly after the occasion of a lecture Dell remembered only too well. They had been at Radcliffe College, in Massachusetts, for three weeks. There had been a girl— Sally, Dell remembered, a dark-eyed, curly-haired girl, very pretty. A graduate student. Rhys had picked her up at a lecture, exercising his considerable charm, and leading her on a whirlwind courtship. He'd asked her to marry him, lightly, in a way seldom taken seriously by anyone—certainly not by himself, and certainly not by Dell, who had witnessed the same chain of events in several cities across the United States. Even the girl, who was not without experience, had accepted it, in the way of the current generation, as little more than a stormy flirtation, a lighthearted and passing romance.

On the day of the lecture, Rhys had been drinking heavily; the girl too; and they had quarrelled. Despite that, the lecture would have been a success—Rhys, even drunk, could be very amusing: moreover, people had almost come to expect it of him—except for one thing. Shortly after the lecture started, Sally had slipped away from her seat in the front row. Rhys had seen her leave, and more, he had seen her leave with another man. After that he had become quite incoherent and vindictive. Eventually he had had to be led from the podium (by me! remembered Dell squeamishly), and sobered up with a succession of black coffees and cold compresses.

It was true, Rhys had felt suicidal for a couple of days. He had had a dreadful hangover, for one thing, and the girl had not returned that night, nor the next. But Rhys had found her eventually, in a bar, and used his irresistible—to others—charm to woo her back. The affair had resumed, no less stormy than before ... and a week later Rhys had been dead.

It had been in a rented car; Rhys, as usual, inebriated beyond the bounds of control, and as usual travelling at breakneck speed. Quite possibly he had fallen asleep at the wheel of the car. He used to fall asleep at the most improbable times.

A self-induced death, yes. But Dell didn't believe it was deliberate.

The letter was maddeningly incoherent. But it *did* refer to his fiancée, if not by name. And it *did* talk of her infidelity, and it *did* rage over his despair with life, his utter despondency. No wonder Raoul had believed her responsible!

Dell sighed and picked up the key, still lying where Raoul had tossed it on the top of the table. She'd come back later, with a mop and duster, and see what could be done about the state of the room. Perhaps Ernestine could find her some more comfortable furnishings ... a chair or two, perhaps a rug to lend a modicum of comfort to the surroundings. In any case, it would be hard to start with any degree of seriousness until she had a typewriter. Raoul had, at least, promised that.

She closed the door carefully behind her. The key grated in the lock; it was rusty from disuse and she would have to remember to oil it sometime. Then she made her way back to the main hall of the château. She felt the churning of her stomach as she rounded each corner of the dim hallway: would he be there?

Perhaps it was just the hunger, after all. Raoul was nowhere in sight, and the amiable bundle of white that emerged from the kitchen was Ernestine. The older woman grinned good-naturedly at Dell, and it lent a touch of sanity to the day.

'Ah, *mademoiselle*! We thought you 'ad forgotten the necessity of eating. But your meal awaits you—a little cold turkey, *non*? It would be good.'

There seemed to be a great deal more than cold turkey piled on the sideboard ... delicious pâtés, hearts of artichoke in a vinaigrette sauce, a fragrant *ratatouille* of eggplant and tomato, lightly touched with spices.

Dell settled herself at the table self-consciously, aware that Ernestine's probing eyes were surveying her with sudden concern.

Mademoiselle is feeling a litle badly, still, from the accident on the road this morning?' It was a kind curiosity after all, and one couldn't take offence. 'Mademoiselle is very pale.'

'I'm fine, Ernestine, really I am.'

'I do not think so.' Ernestine's penetrating gaze swept Dell's face, missing nothing.

'Er—well, perhaps I was a little more shaken up than I realised at the time.' Oh, why, thought Dell, did Ernestine have to be so observant! 'It's very good of you to worry so, but really I'm all right. Not even a bruise to show for it!'

'Mademoiselle is lucky the face 'as escaped!' Ernestine pursed her lips, a small look of worry skimming through her eyes. 'There is just one little mark ...' Her finger crooked itself towards the line of bone beside

Dell's ear, where the imprint of Raoul's thumb must still be showing.

So Raoul had left his mark upon her clearly. Dell felt a wave of mortification.

Ernestine shrugged, doubt apparent in her sharp bird-like eyes. 'Per'aps I should 'ave insisted this morning that you lie down.' She frowned in puzzlement and concern. 'It is strange that I 'ave not noticed earlier this paleness and ... Per'aps you have the concussion?'

'You were too busy looking at my shoes and pantyhose this morning, Ernestine. Really, I'm all right.' Dell busied herself with a mound of pâté and a slab of crusty French bread. 'My only problem is hunger.' She gave a brief embarrassed laugh.

Still Ernestine hovered and clucked like a broody hen, worry pecking at the edges of her mind. 'Monsieur Raoul, 'e would not like it if I did not look after you.'

'Monsieur Raoul is perfectly aware that I fell this morning and he's not worried at all.' The words came more sharply than Dell had intended, and she turned to Ernestine with a half-smile to soften their impact.

Then a small light dawned in Ernestine's eyes. 'Ah, per'aps that is why Monsieur Raoul goes off so fast in the car, without even a word, without even lunch. I think it may be he will fetch the doctor ...?'

'No, Ernestine, he won't.' Dell spoke emphatically. 'He knows I'm fine. Now stop worrying.'

Ernestine looked dubious. 'But Mademoiselle will lie down after the lunch, yes? You promise?'

'All right, Ernestine, if it makes you feel better.' Ernestine seemed satisfied at last with Dell's promise: and to tell the truth, Dell herself felt a little relieved at the idea of a rest. Perhaps it would restore her after the emotional turmoil of the morning.

It was late afternoon when she opened her eyes. She had a distinct sense of disorientation: she was not accustomed to sleeping during the day, and it took her a moment or two to remember where she was.

Already the shadows were lengthening in the courtyard; nightfall was not so very far away. It was time to dress for dinner. She scrambled out of bed and slipped out of her jeans and shirt. She must indeed have been tired; she hated sleeping in her clothes.

The bath was soothing, a balm to the nerves and a restoration to reality. It had been a difficult morning, but it was not the end of the world, and with the resilience of youth Dell found her spirits rising. She scented the bath lavishly with some expensive bath salts that stood by the edge of the tub in a heavy cut glass decanter. Then she towelled herself vigorously and chose her outfit for the evening: a simple, fluid black sheath of clinging silk, skilfully cut to skim her hips and fall into a soft swirl of fabric about her feet. The high neck was accentuated by a large Peter Pan collar of starched white organza, and a wide cuff of the same material edged the long sleeves.

Not that it would change anybody's mind about her —wondering suddenly whether by 'anybody' she really meant Raoul—but at least no one could accuse her of being risqué in her choice of wardrobe. She winced at the remembrance of the hatred that had blazed in his eyes this morning.

Downstairs, the living room was empty. Madame de Briand had not yet descended for dinner. Dell moved across the room to the exquisite inlaid cabinet where

she had seen Raoul prepare drinks yesterday, and
poured herself a measure of Dubonnet. Liquid cour-
age! Perhaps it would give her the fortitude to face
Raoul again.

With her glass in one hand, she walked over to the
collection of paintings on the far wall. This must be a
Braque, she decided. Then an interesting Turneresque
sunset over water, almost contemporary in its simplicity: no signature. Then one that might have been
a Picasso in his Blue Period ... Dell wished she knew
more about art. It was fascinating how the paintings
had been grouped, a mingling of schools, the new and
the old blended with absolute certainty and a fine eye
for balance. Grudgingly she admitted to herself that it
must be Raoul's doing.

She moved along the wall, drinking in its offerings as
she sipped at her Dubonnet. It was a collection that
would do justice to a small museum. She paused before a particularly fine, large portrait. It was of
Madame de Briand. One couldn't mistake those
superb bones, although in the portrait the hair was
still dark and the eyes danced with life. The portrait
had a haunting beauty about it, a beauty more of the
spirit than of the flesh, as if the artist had seen beyond
the surface symmetries and caught, on his canvas, the
living woman. Eugénie de Briand was wearing a dress
of softly draped silk, a vibrant cerulean blue colour,
against which a heavy triple strand of pearls lay like
drops of thick cream, echoing the pale perfection of
skin and colouring. Yet she had not been a young
woman when it was painted—fifteen years before?
Dell was sure she recognised the hand of the artist

and to confirm her guess she peered at the signature, but it was illegible.

'A Saint-Just.' The voice came from behind her, faintly mocking and infuriating as ever. Dell whirled around with a clutch of alarm. How had he arrived so silently?

Raoul moved across to the drinks cabinet. 'I see you've started in already.' He poured himself a generous brandy.

Dell tilted her glass and drained the portion that remained. 'I'll have another. Dubonnet, please,' she levelled at him in a cool voice that said nothing of the disorder of her senses.

For answer he notched one dark eyebrow quizzically and reached for her glass. Dell watched irritably as the dark liquid rose and shimmered against the wall of cut crystal. She was annoyed with herself: she hadn't really wanted another drink.

He handed her the Dubonnet, his hand remaining on the glass for a fraction longer than necessary as she took it from his fingers. There was an awkward pause, a tension between them that was compounded of their memories of the morning.

Then he broke the silence. 'You were discovering our collection.' At last they were on safe ground.

'Yes,' she answered, relief spilling into her voice and giving it more warmth than she intended. 'The portrait of your mother ...'

'Painted before the illness that robbed her of her sight,' he offered.

'She was—is—a lovely woman.' Dell walked back towards the portrait, absorbing its purity of line, something in the expression that seemed almost alive. 'I've

heard of Saint-Just, of course. He's caught her beautifully.'

'One of his better efforts.' Raoul's voice held a note
of dry amusement.

'I know he paints only women he considers to be
truly beautiful.'

'She is that.' They both looked at the portrait in
silence, for once in agreement.

'How—how did it happen? Her blindness, that is?'
Dell pursued the question as she turned away reluctantly from the painting and returned to the fireplace.

'A fever. An infection of the kidney, complicated by
worry—over Rhys. Then a mild stroke; she has never
been a well woman since. It happened eleven years
ago.'

Eleven years ago. Rhys would have been no more
than eighteen then; he had been twenty-nine when he
died. So he had been difficult, even in those days.

And Raoul was older ... how much older? Five, six
years? She glanced at him, measuring. The harsh
angularity of his face wore a musing softness of expression she hadn't seen before. For a moment he looked
younger, Rhys' age.

'Did Rhys live here, then?' Dell let her voice tread
softly into what might be dangerous territory. The
love life of Madame de Briand was common knowledge, but Dell had no idea how it had affected her
family arrangements.

Raoul looked at her with mild surprise, an eyebrow
quirked. 'Rhys confided in you very little, didn't he,
considering ...?' His voice trailed into silence.

'Don't tell me if you'd rather not.'

Raoul shrugged. 'Rhys lived here, yes. Had done,

ever since he was a small lad. This château was never my father's: it has belonged in my mother's family for generations. My mother left my father when I was six years old.'

And if Rhys was born shortly after that, Dell calculated rapidly, Raoul must be about—thirty-six?

'My father was a harsh man, cruel even, and I never blamed her,' continued Raoul, 'not even as a young child. He had collaborated with the Vichy government during the war and my mother never forgave him. He refused to give her a divorce. She took me with her to England, put me in a good school.' So she had not abandoned him, after all.

Raoul stood up and paced moodily in front of the fireplace. 'It wasn't until several years later that I understood what had happened. Her love affair with Emlyn Morgan may have been the most celebrated affair of its time, but to me my mother was just that— a mother. And he was her friend, a warm, kind, sensitive man, who worshipped her and gave her all the love she had never had from my father. It seemed the most natural thing in the world when Rhys was born.' He paused. 'Oh, there were the usual jealousies—sibling rivalry, all that. But having a younger brother was an exciting new world for me to explore, and when Emlyn Morgan died my mother brought us both back here to live. I was twelve at the time. Rhys was five. We were brought up together for seven years, until I moved to Paris. Most of my memories of adolescence were mixed up with Rhys—a cussed, charming, undisciplined little beggar even then.'

Dell smiled; it sounded so much like the Rhys she had known.

'She spoiled him, you know, heaven help her. Rhys always knew exactly what he wanted.' Raoul looked down at Dell, a scowl heavy on his brow. She knew his mind had cut across time to more recent events—her own supposed involvement with Rhys. '... And he usually got it.'

Just then the door opened, and Raoul swung around to greet his mother. A patient Ernestine led Madame de Briand across the room, steering her clear of impediments and not leaving the room until after Madame de Briand was settled into a large armchair. Raoul moved around behind his mother, placing an affectionate hand on her shoulder. She raised her own to grip his in greeting.

'Ernestine has been telling me that there was almost a—a terrible accident today, Raoul. That Dell was quite badly shaken up.' Raoul's eyes sought Dell's from behind his mother's back. There was a warning implicit in them and Dell thought she recognised the message: don't upset her.

'It was nothing ...' Dell broke in, 'a tumble, no more. I scraped my shins. My pantyhose suffered more than I did.' She forced a light laugh.

'Dell is perfectly all right,' agreed Raoul.

'But Raoul, you should have called the doctor.' The blind eyes turned towards her unseen son. 'One must take care; Dell is our guest. A concussion, who knows ...' Madame de Briand seemed genuinely concerned.

'She's a healthy animal,' Raoul countered, his eyes still fixed on Dell.

'Ernestine thought you had gone for the doctor this afternoon. But instead,' Madame de Briand shook her head accusingly, 'instead you went shopping. What could possibly take you shopping today?'

Raoul shrugged. 'Errands ... some little things. It was necessary.'

Madame de Briand pulled her mouth into a disapproving line. 'Ernestine told me there were many large parcels—like Christmas.'

'Ernestine tells you too much,' laughed Raoul.

'She is my eyes,' said Madame de Briand simply, with an almost childish ingenuousness. 'And as she is my eyes, she tells me to worry about Dell. Ernestine said you were most pale at lunch today, Dell, and your face bruised by the fall.'

Dell's hand stole up to her throat and stayed there, in a defensive gesture against the memory of what had transpired in the turret room. She prayed silently that Eugénie de Briand would ask no more questions. Raoul's eyes followed her hand and stayed fastened at her neck, seemingly riveted by the puritanical white of her collar.

'I was—perhaps—a little pale,' agreed Dell hastily, 'but it was part hunger, part tiredness. Really, it was nerves more than anything else. I slept all afternoon and now I feel fine.'

'Ah, you will never tell me the truth. You are one of those uncomplaining types.' Raoul's mother shifted her shoulders and tilted back towards her son. 'Raoul, you must tell me. Is she still pale?'

Raoul looked at Dell, lips pursed, lids lazy over enigmatic eyes; and Dell felt a rush of colour rise to her cheeks. Raoul let a ghost of a smile play about his lips. 'No,' he answered truthfully, 'she's not pale.'

Madame de Briand seemed to relax somewhat. '*Eh*

bien, Dell, at least you had the sense to sleep this after-noon, instead of starting on the sorting of papers. It is as well. There is no haste in this matter.'

'Except as far as my uncle's concerned!' Dell re-marked. 'He's very anxious to publish another Rhys Morgan book as soon as possible. I'll have to start working on it seriously, tomorrow.'

'But you must not rush at it. You are too eager to be finished!' Madame de Briand sounded half amused. 'There is so much else to be done. One cannot work all the time. You must enjoy the Massif Central while you are here.'

'I intend to,' replied Dell promptly.

'You can drive?' demanded the older woman.

'Yes—but I'm not very good on directions,' laughed the girl.

'You may take the Renault when you wish, but you must ask Gaspard for a map. It is an old car, but adequate. We do not believe in this business of a new car every year.'

'That's very good of you.'

'Perhaps Raoul will take you sightseeing, shopping some day,' Eugénie de Briand continued kindly. 'Le Puy is not far from here, a day's expedition, and it is a delightful town. It is in the valley of the Haute-Loire. Yes, you must see Le Puy. Raoul will arrange it; he has business there often. Every week or two.'

'I couldn't ...'

'I can't ...'

The two voices started in unison, Dell's and Raoul's, simultaneously protesting Madame de Briand's suggestion. The blind woman frowned slightly, as if measuring their response, then brightened and added: 'But of course! Ernestine tells me, Dell, that your walking shoes were destroyed this morning, beyond repair. One cannot enjoy the Massif without a sensible pair of walking shoes. You must take her, Raoul, for a day's shopping, or we shall be responsible for ruining her feet.'

Dell opened her mouth, as if to protest further, but Eugénie de Briand had already raised her hand to be led into dinner. The matter was closed.

It was no longer a suggestion; it was an edict.

CHAPTER SIX

THE bed, as Dell slipped from its side, was a tangled testimony to the restless night she had spent. How was she going to tell the truth to Eugénie de Briand?— the truth about herself, the truth about Rhys? For she had decided that she must tell the truth, and soon, even though it would undoubtedly put paid to any chance of publishing the remainder of Rhys Morgan's poetry. She knew she would be disappointing her uncle, and a public hungry for more words from their dead idol. All the same, it must be done. *Dell Everett, married to her job, for better or for worse.* But this time it was for worse; a marriage that put her in such an impossible position was no marriage at all.

Last night's dinner had been a torment. All evening Dell had had the overpowering desire to blurt out the facts of her life, but always there had been Raoul's mocking presence, making the confidence impossible.

How to tell Madame de Briand ... what to tell her ... and when to tell her: those were the questions. It seemed it was going to be difficult, if not impossible, to see the older woman alone. There was always Ernestine, or Raoul. She couldn't bear the thought of discussing her love life, or lack of it, in front of Raoul ... the very thought of his eyes, jeering, glinting again with disbelief as she protested her innocence. No, there was no point in speaking to Madame de Briand while Raoul was present.

Perhaps it was kinder to let Eugénie de Briand continue to believe what she would about herself and Rhys. Strangely, the notion of their involvement seemed to give her comfort. But Dell had become too fond of Madame de Briand to want to live the deception any longer. Or perhaps there was some deeper reason, some other need for confession, some compulsion for baring the soul.

Whatever the reason, it would be good to rid herself of this millstone of lies. She'd do it as soon as possible—that night, she resolved.

The decision made, she felt a lifting of the burden and felt almost lighthearted.

She splashed her face, polished her teeth until they felt smooth as glass to the tip of her tongue, and attacked her hair with a joyful ferocity until it fairly crackled under the onslaught of the brush. All in all, it was a good decision. She made an impudent face at her reflection in the mirror.

Suddenly her eye caught the faint reddish mark that scored her cheekbone. Raoul's imprint. Now it was barely visible. The recollection of yesterday's events flooded back to her with an uncanny clarity. She lifted her hand and let it linger against her cheek, then dropped it to touch her throat, lightly. Once more she could nearly feel his fingers encircling her neck ... the strange weakness, almost a lassitude, that had throbbed through her lower limbs and robbed her of the spirit to resist.

Impatiently she turned away from the mirror, willing herself to thrust the memory from her mind. She was not going to let thoughts of Raoul cast a pall over the day.

From her wardrobe she chose a pale grey turtleneck, pairing it with slacks of a darker grey cord. Then, for a touch of colour, she tucked an oversize red scarf into the narrow belt at her waist. Almost as an afterthought, she pocketed the key to the turret room—*the* room, it was becoming in her mind—and hurried down to breakfast. She had slept unusually late after her night of mental turmoil, and it was time to get to work.

Moments after Dell arrived in the small dining room, a plate of freshly made buckwheat pancakes emerged from the kitchen—*bourials*, Ernestine explained, to be eaten with the sweet local honey. Freshly squeezed orange juice and a steaming cup of coffee completed the morning meal.

After breakfast she made her way to the room in the turret. The key turned more easily in the lock today. Somebody must have oiled it—but who?'

When she opened the door she could hardly believe her eyes. Several floor lamps had been brought into the room, and they were already switched on, bathing the surroundings in a warm glow. On the floor lay a thick, inviting shag carpet that must have been brought from another room in the château, its tawny russets lending a friendly touch of casual comfort. A pair of cosy tapestry armchairs too: those had been stolen from Raoul's own study, Dell thought. The heavy oak table had been dusted and polished. So Raoul *had* let Ernestine come in after all, probably under his own eagle eye. The litter of correspondence had been cleaned away, and a brighter desk lamp installed. The cardboard cartons and envelopes that had stood against the far wall had been moved for cleaning, and now stood in a less noticeable corner of the room. And on the small solid table Dell had moved into place for use as a typing table, there stood a new electric typewriter.

Raoul had done all this for her, in spite of what he thought of her! He must have worked half the night! Perhaps he had some redeeming qualities after all, decided Dell, remembering with contrition the hatred that had raged·in her soul only yesterday. The room was far from perfect, yet, but at least it was habitable. And Raoul had done it all!

So this was what he had been planning when he went shopping yesterday. He had thought of everything: there even a box of fresh typewriter paper. She took a sheet and tested it in the new machine: perfect. Then she sighed and pushed up her sleeves. Work had to be done and she mustn't put it off any longer.

She took one of the large envelopes from the pile in the corner and spilled its contents over the surface of the table. Then she spent perhaps half an hour sorting the things that Rhys had written. This was an old envelope, mailed to Montperdu about eight years before, according to the postmark, and not up to the standard of his more recent writings. Dell found her concentration wavering. For the tenth time she caught herself with her chin propped on her hands, staring distractedly at nothing, and seeing ...

Yes, it was true. Her mind kept returning to Raoul's face, to his eyes, to the chiselled definition of his mouth, to the hard masculinity of him. Why did she have to think of him! That the eyes were cruel, or enigmatic, or scornful; that the mouth was bitter, or mocking, or sardonic—these things seemed to make no

difference. He had carved a notch in her consciousness and refused to be dislodged.

She pushed the papers aside restlessly. This was no
good. Perhaps it was merely guilty conscience for her
previous antagonistic feelings towards Raoul. After
all, he *had* refurbished this room for her. And he *had*
been less vindictive towards her last night, before
dinner. He might be softening. Perhaps she could find
him, thank him, make some amends for yesterday, and
come to some kind of comfortable terms with him.

She swirled her chair around—he had even found
her a swivel chair—and switched off several of the
lights. Rhys could wait another half hour; he had all
eternity. Her uncle, too, could wait.

She picked her way through the gloom of the hall in
search of anyone who could tell her where Raoul might
be found. Ernestine was in the salon, arranging a
bowl of flowers with more enthusiasm than artistry.

'Monsieur Raoul, 'e is in his studio, painting! He
will stop only for meals, and even those 'e will forget, if
I do not bring them. It is best not to disturb.'

'I'll take that chance,' said Dell firmly

Ernestine spread her palms in a gesture of resigna-
tion. 'If Mademoiselle insists ...'

'Where do I find the studio, Ernestine?' asked Dell
equably.

'Ah! Mademoiselle does not know? It is in the
stable, which has been made over—converted, you
understand?'

The stable! What a dingy place to have a studio, reflected Dell, and probably chilly too, even though the
warmth of May was finally permeating the mountain
air. She returned to her room and fetched a heavy red

wool cardigan sweater before leaving the château.

There was no answer when she knocked at the stable door. No windows at all: it was impossible to see whether Raoul was inside or not. She knocked again, loudly. This time, when nobody came, she turned the handle and gave the door a light push.

Inside, the stable was flooded with natural light and Dell gasped with astonishment and pleasure. The entire ceiling of the large room had been inset with a series of curved skylights, giving the space a sense of height and openness, despite the lack of windows. A litter of canvases and frames were stacked face-inward against the walls. There was a long low trestle table, really a wide bench, unfinished, on one side of the room. Its raw wood surface was scattered with assorted equipment—oil paints, turpentine, linseed oil, a large array of clean brushes fanning from a clay flowerpot; some sketchpads; and a scattering of sketches on loose pieces of paper.

Raoul stood across the room at a large easel. As she entered, he looked up, his concentration broken, a frown gathering darkly over his brow. His eyes narrowed ominously. 'What are *you* doing here?'

'I—I came to say thank you.' Back at square one, thought Dell, regretting her decision to interrupt him. She felt her mouth go dry.

He put his brush and palette down on the worktable, rage apparent in every harsh angle of his face. 'Don't you ever knock?'

'I *did* knock,' retorted Dell defensively.

'And do you always butt right in, when there's no answer?'

'No—that is——'

'When I'm painting I don't like to be disturbed.'

'Then when you're painting you should lock the door,' said Dell, reasonably enough.

'I usually do.' He strode to the entrance and twisted the key vehemently.

'Hadn't you better let me out first?' Dell found herself suppressing a laugh despite the thunderous expression on Raoul's face. It was like locking the barn door after the horse had—but no, the horse was inside this time. The simile didn't quite work.

Raoul leaned against the door frame and folded his arms. 'First tell me why you came here.'

'I told you—I came to say thank you.'

'Thank you—for what?' His voice was deliberately cutting.

'For fixing up the room for me.'

'I wouldn't have put a dog to work in that room,' he answered frostily. 'It had nothing to do with you.'

'You went to a lot of trouble.' It was becoming harder to maintain a façade of equanimity; Raoul was hardly a receptive audience.

'OK. Thanks duly noted. Now what else?'

'What do you mean, what else?'

'What else do you want to talk about?'

'Nothing!' Dell was genuinely surprised.

'You had something on your mind last night.' How could he have guessed? Sometimes the man had an uncanny way of getting inside her subconscious.

'I—I don't know what you're talking about,' she said evasively.

'You're lying about something,' Raoul continued with disconcerting insight, 'and I know it. You may as well tell me now.'

'I'm not,' said Dell hotly, turning away with a lowering of the lashes so that he would not see the truth in her eyes.

'As you please,' he shrugged unconcernedly, 'but the door stays locked until I find out. I don't want any more unpleasant surprises.' He jerked the key from the door and hung it on a hook, high above her reach.

'In that case,' she said with a tight smile that barely concealed the frustration that was mounting within her, 'I'll just wait.'

She turned and strolled languidly towards the easel. She could make herself quite at home, thank you. The room was really quite warm, after all: she stripped off the red cardigan and laid it carelessly over the edge of the workbench. Then an indolent stretch of her arms ... he'd soon regret his ultimatum.

She ambled further, to the other side of the easel, totally conscious of the eyes that followed her, yet refusing to acknowledge them. The picture on the easel was barely started, a blocking in of spaces, a definition of lines about the face of the portrait. Dell gave a little start of recognition. Not for the face: it was of a dark-haired woman, perhaps twenty-nine or thirty years old, remarkably beautiful, although Dell had a feeling she wouldn't like her.

What she did recognise was the artist who had painted the portrait.

She turned slowly to face Raoul, her eyes round with surprise and a sense of awe. 'You're Saint-Just,' she said, with absolute certainty.

'True.' A faint mockery of a smile twisted his lip.

'But the name——?' Then she remembered the village of Saint-Just-sur-Haute, where her train had arrived. 'But of course! You took it from the village.'

'Actually, they took their name from us. The Saint-Just family.'

'But——'

'My mother's family. The Saint-Justs have owned this château since the sixteenth century.'

'And you——'

'Raoul Etienne de Saint-Just de Briand.' The name was so pretentious in its entirety that Dell laughed outright.

Raoul smiled sardonically and moved across the room towards the easel. 'I seem to have amused you.'

'It's just that it sounds so—noble. And to think I thought you were a—a——'

'A peasant? I believe that's what you said the first night.' A curl of amusement gave her a glint of even white teeth. 'I am, at heart.'

'I should have thought an important portrait painter would have a shortage of subjects in a place like this.'

Raoul lifted an eyebrow. 'I have a studio in Paris, too. Usually I spend a good part of the year there. In any case there is no shortage of beautiful women in the Auvergne. The Auvergnats have their own kind of beauty.'

'No, I didn't mean that—I mean, commissions.'

'I don't work on commission. I paint only whom I choose,' he added autocratically.

It was true; Dell had heard that. Only women he considered to be truly beautiful, in their own way.

She looked back at the portrait standing on the easel. Yes, the woman was certainly beautiful, she admitted grudgingly, even though the eyes had an unpleasant hauteur and the mouth a small, petulant suggestion of vanity. Raoul at least must enjoy the woman's particular kind of beauty, or he would not be painting her. She felt a twinge of envy.

'Don't you need the person here when you're working on a portrait?'

Raoul shrugged carelessly. 'I don't work that way. I do sketches, studies, colour notes, impressions ... then I start on the portrait. Sometimes it's easier to paint the soul of a person if they're not present.' He studied the canvas with a little frown of dissatisfaction. 'Sometimes —it can be distracting, when a person is here in the flesh.'

'I can imagine,' said Dell not without sarcasm, although she managed a smile. Then, feigning indifference in hopes that he might let her go, she added: 'I suppose you'd like to get back to your work now.'

'I'm in no hurry. It wasn't coming along quite the way I expected.' He pulled a pack of Gitanes from the pocket of his shirt. It was a faded bronze cotton, Dell noted, sleeves rolled up to reveal forearms strong and supple as she had known they would be. The shirt was open to the middle button, revealing a dark tangle of hair: Dell had an urge to sink her fingers in it and tug. A flat stomach; narrow hips; and cream-coloured cotton pants, well-worn and bearing the coloured evidence of his profession.

'Cigarette?' he offered as an afterthought.

'I don't smoke,' said Dell, a little too primly, but there was something about the man that annoyed her, made her feel restless.

'None of the *minor* vices, eh?' There was no mistaking the caustic emphasis of the words and Dell felt an urge to join swords with him. Why should she always be on the receiving end?

'And *you*, of course, are a puritan,' was her cool rejoinder.

'No. Why should I be?' he answered with brutal frankness, 'There are always women like you around.'

Dell jabbed her thumb angrily in the direction of the portrait. '*Her*, for instance?'

'Yes, her.' He was clearly amused now; damn him! He probably felt he was getting the better of the exchange.

'I don't like her looks.' If she couldn't insult him maybe she could insult his taste in women. There must be some way to get beneath that infuriating rhinoceros hide of his!

He flashed her a grin. 'Jealous?'

Why, he's laughing at me, Dell realised, beside herself with rage.

'Why! You conceited, detestable ...' Her hand flashed forward in an involuntary gesture, ready to make stinging contact with his face. No man had ever aroused her to such a pitch of anger!

His hands shot out with rapier swiftness and grasped her wrists, as easily as they might have grasped a naughty child. Dell winced with frustration. It was as though she had run up against a cataclysmic force. She raised one foot and kicked him on the shins, sharply.

'You little bitch!' He flung the words at her, his teeth bared. Then, still grasping her wrists, he twisted her, expertly, so that she was forced into a one hundred and eighty degree turn. Her arms were pulled tightly around her body and she was trapped, defenceless, against the rock-hardness of him.

For a time she struggled, but the more violently she resisted the more her arms pained and the more tightly she seemed to be trapped. After a few moments she became still, her only conscious movement the wild pounding of her heart. His body pressed so closely against her back that she could feel the ripple of every muscle, the tension of every tendon, and his mouth was so near it seemed to stir in her hair ...

'Now will you tell me why you came in here?' His voice was very quiet and all the more dangerous for it.

'I told you——' gasped Dell, 'to thank you. Though God knows why.'

'The truth!' His words held a veiled threat, and he tightened his grip on her. She winced.

'I didn't come for any other reason.'

'You were hiding something last night.'

'No——'

'Tell me.' Another tightening of the hold.

Dell expelled the air that had been searing her lungs, and the words tumbled out. 'I was wondering how to tell your mother the truth about myself and —Rhys.'

Very slowly his grip relaxed, and he moved his hands to her shoulders, turning her body to face his own. His expression was grave.

'What do you mean, the truth? I warned you she must never learn——'

'No; I don't mean the—the—what you call suicide.' Her lashes feathered downward. 'I mean that Rhys and I—we never planned to be married. I tried to tell you yesterday. There was no real engagement.'

He was standing very close, disconcertingly close, his

hands still gripping her shoulders. Then: 'Was there, ever?'

'No,' she whispered, 'never.'

'You must never tell her.' His words ground out harshly from between clenched teeth. 'If you tell her, it will kill her. And surely you already have enough blood on your conscience.'

'I—you just won't understand, will you!' Dell's eyes stung with the frustration of being unable to explain.

'I understand more than you think,' he said frigidly. 'And I have no wish to discuss your love life with Rhys. But as far as my mother's concerned, you will tell her nothing. Nothing!'

'But——'

'Haven't you done enough already? Leave it be. Leave her her dreams.'

Dell felt a chilling shiver invade her body, radiating from the deep pressure of his fingertips on the flesh of her shoulders, down through her limbs. She opened her mouth as if to say more. But why *was* it so important to her that Madame de Briand should know the whole truth and nothing but the truth? Why this fierce desire to put an end to lies and half-lies; why this compulsion to confess? And to confess—what? A lack of sin? And who was it she wanted to tell, anyway? Madame de Briand—or Raoul?

Suddenly she felt confused, unsure of her own emotions and motives.

'I'm sorry,' she said, letting her lashes fall to veil her confusion. Strange, how her life seemed to have turned into an apology for an affair she had never had. And still, the truth of it all trembled on her lips, held back only by her unwillingness to see the expression of mocking disbelief return to his face. She had tried to tell him yesterday and what had he said? *You killed him* ...

It all seemed so unfair, so undeserved! She, Dell Everett, who had never done anything to Rhys Morgan except to try and help him.

The tears that had been building inside her for the last two days could no longer be contained. They spilled out, coursing down her face. She tried to turn away, ashamed of her weakness, but Raoul's grip restrained her. What was this terrible frailty that had seized her body, sapped her strength ... this debilitation of the defences? Dell had always hated to cry. But to cry in front of this man! At least with the tears swimming through her vision it was impossible to see the scorn that must be in his eyes.

His hand moved to her chin with a rough gentleness and tilted her face upward towards his own. She squeezed her eyes closed, trying desperately to staunch the flow, and could feel her chin go rigid with the effort.

'Delilah.' His voice breathed hoarsely against her cheek, so close she could feel the feathering of his lips, the wetness of her salt tears brushing against his mouth. She held her breath, as if poised at the edge of a great precipice.

Then suddenly his lips were on hers, savage, seeking, exploring, ravaging: and the ground fell away from beneath her feet.

Raoul's fingers left her chin and buried themselves at the nape of her neck, making a fist in the pale copper of her hair, until her scalp ached with the tearing, compulsive fury of it; drawing her face roughly against his until she felt her senses shattering with the grinding strength of him. His other hand moved around her back, pulling her waist to his, locking her body fiercely to his own. Dell felt her bones shaking within her, her senses exploding with an overload of messages.

She reached a hand towards his chest in a feeble attempt to push him from her, but instead found her traitorous fingers had crept, unbidden, into the opening of his shirt, touching, investigating, raking against the hard ridge of his collarbone ... then lacing themselves into the dark tangle of hair that grew across his chest. She found her lips parting like willed things in answer to his own, inviting exploration, the edge of her teeth pressing deeply into his lips.

His arms were about her now, both of them, half carrying her towards the low trestle table. Roughly, with one hand, he swept aside the litter of oil paints and sketches, and pressed her body against the rough wooden surface. For several moments his limbs crushed her with growing urgency. Then he straightened, and Dell found herself free of him.

She lay perfectly still on the bench, feeling only a trembling enervation, an insane pounding of the heart over which she had no control. He stood above her now, peeling off his shirt. His fingers moved to the buttons of her blouse, beginning to undo them.

'What—what are you doing?' Dell gasped, the cold reality of the situation returning to her.

'What do you think?' His voice was rough.

'Well, stop!'

'Isn't it what you wanted?' His voice was brutal, like

Get your
Harlequin Presents
Home Subscription NOW!

For exciting
details, see special
offer inside.

Printed in U.S.A.

a whiplash against the still tingling disorder of her senses.

Dell flew to her feet. 'You can't——!' She grasped his hands, pulling them away.

'Why not?' He stood arms akimbo, angry now like a rampant lion, the hair of his chest describing a dark Tee against his bronzed skin. 'Your invitation has been loud and clear for two days now.'

'My—invitation!' Dell couldn't believe her ears. 'I wouldn't have *invited* you. Not if you were the last man on earth.'

'No? You prefer the ones who can't see through you —like Rhys?' His lip curled with scorn.

'At least Rhys was kind,' blazed Dell, hating this turbulent dark destroying man.

He stared down at her, an intensely penetrating gaze, and her eyes wavered under it.

Then he stalked over to the door, and reached up for the key. It slipped easily into the lock. Raoul opened the door and stood with one hand resting on it, waiting. Dell walked towards him shakily, clutching at the shreds of her dignity. She paused briefly at the threshold.

'I—I'm sorry,' she said lamely. Again! she writhed.

His eyes were unreadable, and the suggestion of a shrug broke the strained set of his shoulders.

'There's no accounting for tastes,' he said stiffly, and Dell caught the tiny dangerous glint of gold in his eyes.

Then the door closed between them.

CHAPTER SEVEN

THE town of Le Puy lay in the cradle of the valley, soft and slumbrous. Its buildings clustered haphazardly up the steep rise of streets and spilled down into the valley—tawny red-tiled roofs and ochre walls laid out like a three-dimensional tapestry against the reddish purple of distant hills and the new green of trees. Most startling of all were the unexpected formidable cones of lava that lanced through the heart of the town like gnarled guardians of the past—dark volcanic juttings, memories of an elemental violence that had once erupted through the earth's prehistoric crust. The precipitous silhouettes gave the town a shape, a character unlike anything Dell had seen.

From the top of one weird flattened cone rose an enormous statue—a statue of the Virgin, Raoul explained, cast more than a century before from two hundred cannon captured at the Battle of Sevastopol, in the Crimean War. On a lower rise of lava stood the town's famous cathedral, its polychromatic stone tracing an intricate zebra-striped pattern in sweeping Romanesque arches. And on the third peak, most precipitous of all, a high and pointed place halfway between earth and sky, stood a small and superb chapel.

'Saint Michel d'Aiguilhe,' volunteered Raoul, 'Saint Michel of the Needle. Perhaps we'll see it later, after lunch. It takes stamina to climb those steps! There are two hundred and sixty-seven of them.'

'I'd like to try it.' Dell peered eagerly out the open window of the Porsche. The still-cool air was clean and pure, as if washed by mountain springs. Dell felt she could almost taste it. A light mist lay in the valley, giving the town a sense of other worlds, other centuries. She breathed deeply, with a sense of contentment.

Now, she was glad that Madame de Briand had continued to insist on the outing to Le Puy. And although Raoul had resisted the suggestion during this past week, he had finally given in with good enough grace.

It was early yet. They had set off immediately after breakfast and the sun was still fairly low on the horizon. Raoul had been unusually communicative, even charming, this morning—offering information about points of interest along the way; relating local legends; stopping the car once to let Dell admire a particularly fine view of a bridge that spanned the mountains, its steel girders seeming to soar through space with deceptive fairy-tale fragility, an ethereal testimony to the nineteenth century's great era of railway construction.

And now he was planning an itinerary for the day in Le Puy.

'We'll see the cathedral this afternoon, too,' he was saying decisively. 'It's a magnificent structure. There are stories of miracles ... supposedly the cathedral was built on the site of a pagan table stone where a woman was cured of a fever. A white stag is then supposed to have walked around her, marking the outlines of the first cathedral. In the Middle Ages pilgrims came from all over. They still do, every year.'

Dell stole a sidelong glance at her companion. Gone was the intense, near-vicious concentration she had sensed on their previous drives together. Today he was relaxed, handling the wheel easily, a sureness of touch, an almost sensual enjoyment of the power that surged beneath his competent hands. His leisure suit of fawn-coloured suede, worn with a dark brown turtleneck sweater, emphasised the lean hard good looks and the lithe animal grace of him. Today he was making a distinct effort to be good company, and it seemed hard to remain angry with him.

Not that the past week had brought any more of those soul-destroying scenes. Since that day in the studio, Raoul had been polite, remote, with a careful coolness that left Dell feeling she must have imagined that other Raoul—the Raoul of blazing eyes and in-flamed passions. She let a little sigh escape her lips, wishing ... she didn't know what.

'That sounds like a heavy thought,' observed Raoul, a sudden smile breaking his face. How white and strong his teeth are, reflected Dell involuntarily, remembering the taste of him on her lips. This was insane. She didn't even like the man very much.

'Just—dreaming,' she answered, pulling her sweater close about her and giving a little shiver. 'It's that mediaeval look of Le Puy ... rather like stepping into another century.'

'The Greeks, the Gauls, the Romans were all here,' smiled Raoul. 'In fact the town's so old nobody really knows how it got started.' He manoeuvred the car along a narrow street, slowing for a clutch of children who darted with screams of laughter in pursuit of a stray ball.

'Today's market day,' he continued as he wheeled the car deftly into a parking space and switched off the ignition. 'It's quite a sight. And the market-place is only a few streets from here. If you'd like to see it——'

'Oh, yes, please.' Dell's eyes sparkled with anticipation. 'I'd love it.'

For answer Raoul smiled and leaned across to open the passenger door for her. She held her breath momentarily as his arm grazed within millimetres of her waist. A near miss.

She slipped out of the car and shook the stiffness of travel from her legs. She had chosen slacks today, for comfort—a rusty auburn wool, several shades darker than her hair. Over them she wore a heavy angora cardigan coat of the same auburn colour, casually belted at the waist; and under this a navy blue turtleneck sweater. Her hair tumbled over her shoulders, luxuriant and loose, caught by a light spring breeze and teased into tendrils that framed her face softly. She looked cool and young and relaxed.

Raoul waited for her, watching as she rounded the car, a faint smile etched on his mouth. As she reached him he turned in the direction of the market-place and set off, Dell following, vaguely disappointed that he had not offered her his arm. But then he was obviously not a man who coddled women—and Dell, who had always prided herself on her independence, realised with a twist of regret that for once it would be lovely to be coddled.

Soon she understood why they had parked some distance from the market-place. In the square there was a frantic melée of pushcarts, people, pigs and chickens. She saw a leather-jacketed Auvergnat hoist a healthy sow by an ear and a tail: its soprano squeals of protest sounded sharply over the general hubbub.

The colour of the market-place was brilliant. A row

of strawberry stands patched one section of the market with a riot of red; beside that spread a field of green created by carts of cabbages, lettuces, and shallots. Great piles of radishes lay in bulbous bunches. Tubs of fresh butter stood invitingly side-by-side with heavy crocks of honey. In the fish-stands, freshly-caught salmon and trout from the mountain streams were laid out with the artistry of a still-life painting. Then the cheeses: huge cylinders of Cantal, Saint-Gerlon, Amber Saint-Daubin, and finally Roquefort, redolent of the mountains of the Aveyron to the south, and the craggy hillside town that had given it birth.

At the fringes of the market, a little apart from the crush, were the lace-sellers. Raoul guided Dell to the stalls where one could buy almost anything in lace: scarves, squares, collars, small mats, heavy and elaborate tablecloths that must have taken many months to make. Dell fingered the handwork admiringly as Raoul explained that for centuries Le Puy had been the centre of an enormous lace-making industry, a cottage industry, whole mountain communities clicking their bobbins busily through the long snowbound winters.

'A century ago,' he told Dell, 'there were more lace-makers in Le-Puis-en-Velay than in all of Belgium. Then the machines came ... and now,' he shrugged, 'now it is a dying industry.'

'But look at the stalls and stalls of lace! It can't be dying,' Dell exclaimed.

'Tourist bait,' he replied. 'Still made in the cottages around here, but the skill is dying. It's hardly the world trade it once was.'

'I think it's lovely,' answered Dell defiantly, 'so that makes me the typical tourist.' They stood at a stall which, unlike most of the others, sold articles of clothing. Dell held up an exquisite blouse. The champagne lace was fashioned with the lavish attention to detail of another era, a particularly intricate and curious pattern, very heavy and expensive-looking, lending an old-fashioned demureness to the blouse. But the cut was purely twentieth century: long narrow sleeves, very simple, and a neckline that plunged, Dell guessed, beyond the limits of decency. The entire garment had been lined with a soft, fine cotton lawn. Reluctantly she replaced the blouse on the stall, and chose a dainty lace handkerchief to take home for her aunt.

'Now how about those shoes?' said Raoul, turning away from the stall. 'The stores are only a few minutes' walk from here.'

The late May sunshine spilled like liquid over the town, enhancing its amber-and-old-gold agelessness. The boutiques where Raoul led her were clustered together in a row along a steep rise of road, narrow high shuttered buildings built, like most other structures in this part of Le Puy, right to the edge of the street. A discreet sign over the doorway proclaimed one building to be a shoe-shop. Raoul delivered Dell to the doorstep and paused, one foot resting on the rise of the threshold.

'I'll meet you in a couple of hours,' he suggested. 'I have some business to attend to. There's a little café not far from here, on the Boulevard Saint-Louis.'

'You're not staying?' Dell felt a jab of disappointment. Ridiculous; she didn't need him to help her pick a pair of shoes.

'No, why should I?' he said carelessly. And he gave her directions to the café. Dell let her glance trail after him for a few moments as he walked away down the street, very masculine, very sure of himself. There was a small strange constriction of her throat, an unaccountable sense of disappointment.

It was nearly twelve-thirty when she arrived at the café, swinging her purchases in a little net bag—the shoes, some shampoo, a box of chocolate almonds for Madame de Briand, an interesting antique paperweight for her uncle.

Raoul was already waiting in the café, tilted back indolently in his chair, leafing casually through a copy of *La Montagne*. Dell pulled her chair to the table and Raoul folded the newspaper, laying it aside on the chequered tablecloth.

'So. Mission accomplished?' He glanced at Dell, his eyes half concealed behind low lids.

She nodded. 'Nice shops. Although shopping's not my favourite occupation.'

He tilted an incredulous eyebrow. 'I thought it was an obsession with most of your sex.'

'You have a lot to learn about my sex,' countered Dell, with a light laugh.

He seemed amused. 'It seems I do,' he murmured. 'You might start by instructing me about your preferences in food.'

Dell settled for a luncheon of pike quenelles, with a salad of the green lentils for which Le Puy was justly famous; Raoul chose lobster with a truffade of cheese and potatoes. While they ate he talked knowledgeably about a wide variety of subjects, and Dell found the last traces of animosity dissolving in the companionable atmosphere.

'Being an artist must have its advantages,' she remarked as they sipped pungent cups of strong coffee after the meal. 'Work when you feel like it, take a day off when you feel like it, no nine-to-five nonsense.'

'I often work longer hours than that,' Raoul observed equably.

'Why did you decide to paint under the name of Saint-Just? Why not your own name, de Briand?'

'The de Briand name was rather well known a generation ago. My mother, the actress.' He made a deprecatory gesture. 'I didn't want to trade on it. And besides,' he laughed, teeth white and strong in the weathered bronze of his face, 'it was a rather ghoulish joke. A—family affair.'

'Don't let me intrude,' said Dell dryly.

'No secret, I assure you. The name of Saint-Just has been quite—infamous in history.'

'Oh? Why?'

'Mostly because of Louis-Antoine de Saint-Just. During the French Revolution they called him "The Angel of Death". A startlingly handsome young man, by all accounts, and a fanatic disciple of Robespierre.'

'An ancestor of yours?'

'Who knows? Two centuries have passed and time obscures these things. If so, it was a rather unfortunate offshoot of the family tree. Fascinating, nevertheless. He's been called the most enigmatic personality of the entire Revolution.'

Dell creased her brow. 'My history's a little shaky.'

'Strangely enough, he was a stern visionary, a pillar of rectitude.' Raoul paused to light a cigarette. 'He became Robespierre's hatchet man, because he was absolutely cold-blooded, inhumanly so. At the end of the Revolution, when Robespierre and all his henchmen were rounded up for *la guillotine*— dirty, dishevelled, riding miserably to death in the tumbril—Saint-Just was the only one who retained his dignity. They say he rode standing, impassive as marble, his fawn-coloured breeches and white waistcoat absolutely immaculate. Merciless and implacable to the end.'

Dell shivered, remembering the cold glint of fury she had seen in Raoul's eyes a week ago. She wondered if there were more of Raoul's infamous ancestor in him than he cared to admit. 'And why on earth did you choose to use the name?'

Raoul shrugged. 'It amused me. Perhaps to prove that the name Saint-Just need not always be synonymous with inhumanity.'

Raoul ground his half-smoked cigarette into the ashtray. 'Or perhaps,' he continued, 'it was a grudging admiration, in spite of everything. What was that line of Shakespeare's?—"Nothing in his life became him like the leaving it".'

'Rather frightening, all the same.'

Raoul laughed amiably enough, dispelling murky visions of a dim and horrible past. 'It was all a very long time ago. Now, do you still feel up to climbing the Needle?'

'To Saint Michel, you mean?' Dell gathered her purse and her purchases. 'I'm willing, if you are.'

'Good.' He tilted his head towards the net bag. 'First, we'll put those in the car.'

The steps were steep and old and seemingly endless, and Dell was quite breathless by the time they reached the top, although Raoul had insisted they pause to rest several times along the way.

'Well? Was it worth the climb?' he asked.

'Raoul, it's beautiful!' Dell stood entranced.

'The building is over a thousand years old,' Raoul remarked. 'It was built in 962 ... the portal was added two centuries later. Once it was a hermitage—Le Séguret, the place of safety. The monks climbed up never to return to the valley below.'

'That's rather sad. It's beautiful here, halfway between earth and sky, but ... I think I'd miss the people down there.'

'Perhaps the monks did too. Or perhaps they found a kind of peace here ... a peace they hadn't been able to find in the hurly-burly of the world below.'

A light breeze lifted the soft tendrils of Dell's hair and winnowed them across her eyes. She lifted an impatient hand to brush them aside. 'Peace—at any price? I wouldn't buy it.'

Raoul slanted an amused glance in her direction. 'No, I don't think you're the type to go into retreat. I can imagine you more as a courtesan at the court of some Renaissance king ... or even as a fiery Boadicea, hurling your chariot into battle. But as a nun? Never. They'd have to start a whole new order.'

There were only two ways for Dell to react to Raoul's comment—to get angry, or to laugh. And it was too lovely a day to remain on the offensive, so she decided on the latter course. 'Who knows? Maybe I'd make a very good nun.'

'You'd make a very unusual one,' he observed.

'Thanks for the compliment,' she returned, with a toss of auburn hair, and wrinkled her nose at him.

'You should smile more often,' he said unexpectedly. 'It does things for your nose.'

'Which is otherwise quite unremarkable,' Dell quoted him.

'Did I say that?' He shrugged. 'I may have to revise my whole opinion.'

'Don't,' said Dell, jamming her hands deeply into her cardigan pockets. 'It might be too much of a shock to your system.'

He leaned indolently against a stone pillar. 'You give as good as you get, don't you?'

'I don't believe in one-sided relationships,' Dell said firmly. 'A woman doesn't have to be a doormat.'

'Oh no, not one of those.' His tone was almost indulgent. 'Militant femininity on the march.'

'Women's Lib, that's me,' flipped Dell, who'd never given it much thought before in her life.

'Fast and loose, eh? Same rules as for the men?' There was a corrosive edge to his remark.

'I make my own rules,' answered Dell loftily. It was none of his business what those rules were.

'I'll bet you do,' he returned dryly.

'And one of my rules is never to argue morality with a man who obviously has no use for it himself.'

'Now whatever gave you that idea?'

'If you don't know, I'm not going to remind you,' retorted Dell. 'Some things are best forgotten.'

'Really? Including—Rhys?'

Suddenly a cloud seemed to come over the day, although there was none in the sky. The inoffensive swordplay had started to draw blood. Dell shivered, and turned away from Raoul.

There was a moment's silence. Then, 'I'm sorry,' he said softly, and she felt him lay his hand over her arm.

'You never forget for a minute, do you?' Her voice

was bitter, and she shook him away truculently.

'I said I'm sorry.' He spoke with difficulty, as though unused to apologies. But she stubbornly continued to look at the distant hills mounding against the skyline, a turbulent vista of reds and purples and greens.

'Shall I go down on bended knee?' There was a faint, mocking tone in his voice, and Dell found herself capitulating.

'Well, in that case . . .' she said, 'if you do it down all two hundred and—what did you say?—sixty-seven steps.'

'I'll tell you what I'll do.' He grasped her arm. 'I'll make amends by taking you out for dinner on the way back to Montperdu. I know just the place. A delightful little inn, several miles past Saint-Just-sur-Haute.'

'I accept! But isn't it a little early yet?'

'Mmmm. But by the time we've seen the cathedral, done the rest of the boutiques—there are some interesting ones—and driven for two hours, you'll be ready for a good meal. And that's one thing Noëlle does turn out—a good meal.'

'Noëlle?' Dell's voice held a question.

'The woman who runs the inn,' he explained patiently, steering her down the steep steps. 'Noëlle Rossignol. A widow . . . she opens the inn every year about this time, for the summer season.''

Dell had a vision of someone very like Ernestine or Marie-Ange, black dress buried in a snowstorm of white aprons, square capable peasant's hands and wonderful home-cooked meals. The dinner would be something to look forward to.

The sense of anticipation lasted through the afternoon. Raoul guided her expertly through the superb cathedral with its almost Moorish architecture, pointing out the Black Virgin, a statue primitive in its strength and serenity; letting her linger to admire the ornate Bible of Theodolphus, opulent in purple and gold on fine vellum. It was altogether an imposing place, but privately Dell felt she had preferred the stark simplicity of Saint Michel d' Aiguilhe.

The drive through the deepening afternoon was cooling and enjoyable after the strain of so much climbing ... to the Needle, to the cathedral, through the snaking streets of Le Puy. Dell felt pleasurably exhausted from the exertion, yet alert in every fibre. She stretched in the car like a sleepy cat, revelling in the feeling of tired satisfaction.

'Now don't go to sleep on me,' warned Raoul. 'You're fast becoming a typical Auvergnat—early to bed, early to rise.'

'I've noticed everyone gets up with the sun at Montperdu,' remarked Dell. 'Is it the same all over?'

'More so! Shutters close tight, lights go out almost as soon as the sun sets. Perhaps it's a hangover from mediaeval times.'

'Yet there are TV aerials on some of the smallest cottages,' observed Dell. The car was winding past the village of Saint-Just-sur-Haute, and she could see visible proof of the twentieth century outlined here and there against the sky, the faint spidery skeletons of aerials over some of the houses.

'True, times are changing. But the greengrocer still goes through the streets ringing a bell every Tuesday to announce the arrival of a fresh load of produce. And the barber still turns up Saturday night, once a week, regular as clockwork, and sets up shop in the local pub.

The banker still goes around door-to-door every Friday afternoon, knocking to see if anyone has any financial business to attend to. And the postman still wears the leather cap, a sort of insignia of his office, that his father wore before him, and his grandfather and great-grandfather before that.'

About ten minutes past the town of Saint-Just, Raoul steered the car adroitly into a small serpentine dirt road, a bumpy irregular *voie ordinaire* that was little better than a cart-track. 'The inn isn't far from here. Hungry?'

'Starved! I think I could eat a whole roast pig.' And indeed, Dell could feel the pangs gnawing at her.

'Good. You may get it. When I phoned this afternoon I told Noëlle we'd be hungry.' Raoul grinned, a flash of white in the gloom of dusk. 'I think we'll be just in time for dinner.'

The inn was a charming building, a small *manoir* that seemed to have been renovated recently, and with great good taste. Roses climbed over the exterior, their buds about to break through with the coming of summer. A neatly tended vegetable bed stood off to one side, laid like a handkerchief on the one level piece of land nearby.

Raoul parked the Porsche and Dell jumped out, startled to find that for once he had come around the car to help her out. Would wonders never cease!

He gripped her elbow resolutely and led her to the door. Dell found herself thoroughly enjoying the sensation. What was it Madame de Briand had said ... ? Even big girls need a strong hand, now and then. Well, Raoul certainly had a strong hand.

Raoul knocked briefly, and opened the front door

with the assurance of habit, without waiting for an answer. The front hall was dimly lit, and sparsely, but tastefully, furnished. A heavy brass chandelier, an antique umbrella stand, a low bombé chest, and a scattering of Oriental carpets gave the entranceway a studied charm.

'Give me your sweater,' ordered Raoul. 'You won't be needing it. It's warm in the dining room. Although I can't say the same for the rest of the house.'

Dell removed the heavy cardigan and handed it to Raoul, who threw it over the umbrella stand with an air of easy familiarity. Just then a door opened and the figure of a woman emerged into the dimly lit hall. She paused at the threshold, silhouetted darkly against the golden glow of electricity that shone through the doorway.

Raoul moved across to the woman and leaned over, giving her an affectionate kiss on the cheek. For a moment Dell squinted, adjusting her eyesight to the sudden light.

Raoul's arm was about the woman's shoulder now. 'Noëlle, this is Dell. Delilah Everett. You've heard me talk of her. Dell—Noëlle Rossignol.'

With a shock Dell realised it was the woman in the portrait. There was no mistaking it ... except that she was more beautiful, if anything, in the flesh. That hint of selfishness, of petulance, that Dell had glimpsed in the painting was certainly well concealed now. Noëlle Rossignol was small, fine-boned, exquisitely preserved, flawless from the white flutter of her hands to the beautifully coiffed ebony gleam of her hair. Her mouth was a sensual curve of coral and her nose was—well, perfect. Dell felt very large, very raw-boned, very juvenile. And very imperfect.

'H-how do you do?' she stuttered, holding out a hand that for some reason felt slightly damp.

But Noëlle Rossignol seemed not to notice, for she had already turned back to Raoul and was displaying with artful coquetry a row of small faultless teeth. 'But Raoul, *mon cher*, you did not tell me Miss Everett— Delilah—was a redhead! The red hair, it is so striking, *n'est-ce pas?*' She turned back to Dell, who had dropped her hand, and stood seething inwardly. She could call herself a redhead if she wanted, but she hated when other people did. Especially small, sloe-eyed, perfect women with throaty, perfect voices.

'But Miss Everett, you must come in to the salon. You look exhausted! What have you been doing to her, Raoul?' And lacing her arm through his, she led them into the adjoining room. 'Well, Raoul?'

'We've been sightseeing, the usual tourist round in Le Puy,' Raoul answered evenly.

'Then you must have been too zealous, *mon cher!* Delilah looks utterly destroyed.'

'We've been climbing the Needle. We're both a little rumpled,' said Raoul easily.

'But *you* look perfectly fresh, Raoul! Although why you would waste your energy on that climb ...!' Noëlle Rossignol shuddered very delicately. 'I wouldn't do it for *any*body.'

'I enjoyed every minute.' Dell enunciated the words very distinctly so that the two people walking ahead of her stopped and looked back in mild surprise. She felt positively mutinous now, although why she wasn't sure.

Noëlle laughed, a surprised tinkly laugh that

sounded like a fingernail on fine crystal and owed a great deal to artifice. 'But of course you enjoyed yourself, my dear! It goes without saying! One *does*, with Raoul as companion. One is so pampered.'

'Is one?' Dell gave a reasonable imitation of the other woman's laughter, a silvery little peal of retribution. 'One didn't notice.'

Raoul gave her a quick look. 'Put the claws away, Dell. We're Noëlle's guests and she's an old friend of mine.' He spoke to her as he might have done to a rebellious child.

Dell flashed an indignant look in his direction. Tell *her* to put the claws away, would he? And how about that minx of a Frenchwoman?

'I'm sure she is,' she answered with a saccharine smile.

Raoul looked distinctly displeased. With an ingratiating smile Noëlle detached her arm from his and moved to a fine old breakfront that held a selection of bottles.

'You see, Raoul?' she trilled without a ruffle in her satin-smooth composure, 'You *have* exhausted Delilah. She is quite beside herself. She needs a drink, and so do you—it must have been a dreadful day for you.'

And the dreadful part, of course, was me, thought Dell, doing a slow burn.

'Thanks.' If Raoul had sensed the cattiness of Noëlle's remark, it certainly didn't reflect in his tone of voice. 'Scotch on the rocks; I'll look after it.'

He moved over to the breakfront and took over the task of pouring drinks. Quite used to acting the host here, thought Dell viciously, but she kept her silence.

She accepted a sherry without demur, and sat down

on a delicate medallion-back sofa with slender cabriole legs. Elegant, but hardly comfortable, she decided. Raoul threw himself into a deep upholstered wing chair and she wished she had found it first. It looked like the one inviting piece of furniture in the room.

'How good it is to see you, Raoul,' continued Noëlle Rossignol when they had settled themselves. 'It seems an age. You must learn to use the telephone more often, *non*?'

Raoul grimaced. 'An instrument of torture.'

'But a necessary one,' returned Noëlle with a little laugh. 'How else would you have been able to find out today that I was back from Paris?'

'And you're back to stay this time?' Raoul had turned towards Noëlle, paying scant attention to Dell, who sat stiffly on the uncomfortable sofa. 'When does the inn open for the season?'

'Two weeks. But already most of the staff is here ... chef, gardener, maid.' Noëlle stood against the fireplace, her ripe curves outlined against the flickering flames, an arm delicately balanced along the mantelpiece. She was wearing a long dress of peacock blue silk, its artfully supple cut proclaiming its undoubted origin in one of the great fashion houses of Paris.

Dell watched the two of them with growing annoyance, taking cold comfort in the knowledge that Noëlle at least didn't prepare those perfect meals Raoul had mentioned with her own lily-white hands. But it was hard to fault her in any other way. Noëlle Rossignol was a woman who cultivated perfection.

Noëlle directed a question at Raoul. 'This show of your paintings next month—it will be taking you back to Paris soon?'

'No,' returned Raoul. 'Nearly everything's ready now. Most of the canvases are already at the gallery. Those that remain in the studio here will be shipped next week, and I won't go to Paris until the show is being hung.'

'You will be gone long?' demanded Noëlle with a little moue of mock despair.

'Two weeks at the most.' Raoul shrugged carelessly. 'If it were not such an important opening, I would prefer not to be in Paris at all at that time of year. The rest of the summer I shall spend at Montperdu.'

'But that is splendid,' purred Noëlle. 'One can get so lonely in this part of the world when one is ... alone.' There was a small break in her voice, a tiny plea for sympathy. The merry widow, thought Dell vindictively ... or was it the black widow spider?

Raoul pulled a pack of cigarettes from his shirt pocket and tapped two into a hand. Then he lit both simultaneously, rising to hand one to Noëlle.

'May I have a cigarette too?' demanded Dell. Raoul swivelled to look at her with surprise, but he moved over quickly enough and handed her the cigarette that remained in his own hand. Then he returned to the wing chair and lit another.

'Personally, I like being alone,' said Dell in cool reference to Noëlle's earlier comment. 'It gives me a sense of independence. But then,' she drew slowly on the unaccustomed cigarette and let the smoke escape without inhaling, 'some people have so few inner resources.'

Raoul glanced at her from across the low coffee table. 'And some people have so few inhibitions,' he observed coldly.

'I thought we agreed you wouldn't talk about my morals if I didn't talk about yours,' returned Dell airily.

'It's not morals I'm talking about, it's manners,' he replied.

'Mine or yours?' flipped Dell.

'Now, now,' said Noëlle soothingly, electing to act as the peacemaker. 'You really must go in for dinner. Pierre is preparing a *soufflé aux marrons* for dessert and he will be devastated if it is allowed to fall. You will not mind, Raoul,' she trailed a pale coral-tipped finger against his hand, '—you will not mind if I join you? It has been a while ... and as the inn is not yet open ...'

'Of course not.' A smile crinkled his eyes, briefly, and he bowed with exaggerated gallantry. 'I can think of nothing more charming than the prospect of your company.'

'*Alors* ... shall we go? We must proceed with the entrée at once.'

The table had already been set for three. Dell reflected, with a touch of irritation, that Noëlle must have been very sure of her inclusion in the evening. The thought gave her little comfort.

The meal was exquisitely served and prepared to perfection, but the occasion was not altogether comfortable. Dell found herself concentrating as best she could on the delicately flavoured trout and the delicious brace of pheasant, swiming in a heavy sauce laced with cream and cognac. She let the conversation wash over her. Talk of mutual friends whom Dell didn't know; gossip of what was happening in Saint-Just-sur-Haute; discussion of Noëlle's plans for renovating a sunroom at the back of the *manoir*; talk of Paris.

So Raoul saw Noëlle in Paris, too. Of course, he had a studio there, Dell recalled. And Noëlle was only in the Massif Central during the summer months. Obviously the acquaintance was no casual one.

'But, Raoul! You must do something about that studio of yours. It is in entirely the wrong *quartier* of Paris.' Noëlle Rossignol leaned forward towards her dinner companion with maddening intimacy. 'Something more fashionable—I insist upon it.'

Dell looked sidelong at Raoul, who sat with a nonchalant elbow propped against the table, enjoying a demi-tasse and a *ballon* of cognac. She half expected him to tell Noëlle to mind her own business, but he simply smiled, a fleeting enigmatic smile, and swirled the amber liquid against the sides of his glass.

It was then that the truth struck Dell. She, Delilah Everett, was hopelessly, insanely, bitterly jealous.

And she was jealous because she was in love with Raoul de Briand.

CHAPTER EIGHT

'WELL, you made a delightful guest!' Dell could hear the sarcasm in Raoul's voice as the words splintered across the darkness. He was driving with savage concentration, pitting his skill against the night and the narrow twisting road with angry determination.

'I hardly said a word,' she answered stiffly. It was true. After that initial scene in the salon, and the revelation that had dawned on her at dinner, she had murmured only the bare essentials of conversation ... a muffled thanks, a word of goodbye.

'A few words—but not too well chosen.' He swerved the car into the long rock pass leading to Montperdu. The high foreboding walls caught the blaze of headlights and looked angry that their peace, too, had been disturbed. 'Sometimes you can be a real bitch.'

'Yes, I can,' replied Dell with an insouciance she did not feel. No use to remind him that Noëlle Rossignol had been a real bitch too. Noëlle was too clever for Raoul to have noticed that. She felt a hard lump at the base of her throat. She, Dell Everett, who had managed to reach twenty-four years of age heart-whole, no strings attached, who had always prided herself on her independence, now to feel this way about a man who hated her!

The car swung into the courtyard and grated to a half on the cobblestones. Surely there was something she could say, something she could do to restore the companionable spirit of this afternoon.

'Raoul ...' she began, but he had already jack-knifed out of the car, grabbing a small parcel from the floor at the driver's seat. The door slammed behind him. Either he had not heard her pained plea, or he chose to ignore it.

Dell sat in the car, numb and miserable. She heard his retreating shoes ring sharply on the stones. He had gone to his studio: for a moment the light from its doorway clicked on and bathed the courtyard in an eerie yellow glow, then the door slammed, and Dell was alone in the night.

Finis. The end to a day that had started with such promise, a day that would live for ever in her memory, a bittersweet, soul-shattering day. A day that had made a mockery of everything she had ever believed about herself. The self-reliant Miss Everett—thorny and independent, prickly and proud! Reduced to a quivering jellyfish. So spineless that if Raoul had emerged from the stone keep of his studio right now, she knew she would run over and throw herself right into his unreceptive arms.

But Raoul did not emerge and she couldn't sit here all night. Reality had to be faced. Her legs, feeling strangely boneless, slid through the car door, and took her shakily to the door of the château.

The door was locked. Dell lifted the heavy brass knocker, miserably conscious that she would be unable to escape Ernestine's eagle inspection this evening. How she would have preferred to flee to the privacy of her own room without seeing anyone!

But it was Héloise who answered, grinning and bobbing a small excuse for a curtsey. 'Bonsoir, made-

moiselle ... Madame de Briand *vous attend.*' With a deprecating gesture, the young girl indicated that Dell should enter the salon.

Oh no, thought Dell. Usually Eugénie de Briand had retired to her bedroom by this hour. She must have waited up especially to see herself or Raoul. There was nothing for it but to go into the salon and get it over with.

Madame de Briand was sitting by the fireplace, her face averted from the door. Ernestine was beside her on a low stool, reading out loud, and Dell recognised the words: '... when night is blind, with silken limb entwined ...'

They were the words that Rhys had written, words from his last book. To Delilah. Dell stood very still, her breath caught in a tangle of emotions, and waited as Ernestine finished the poem.

As the last words trembled into silence, Madame de Briand turned her face towards the direction where Dell stood, and there was a sheen to her sightless eyes, almost as though tears hesitated on their brink. The older woman held out her hands, pale and frail as the skeletons of autumn leaves, and slowly Dell grasped them with her own, her own eyes filling with the malaise of her soul.

'My dear.' Eugénie de Briand's voice was scarcely louder than a whisper, and there was a curious catch to it. 'You must forgive me. The words have aroused emotions you might think an old woman had better leave forgotten. But you must tell me about your day in Le Puy.'

'I——' Dell stumbled to a halt. She felt too choked with her own purgatory of emotion to continue.

'What is the matter, my dear? You are saying noth-ing.' Madame de Briand leaned towards Dell, her face etched with concern.

'*Elle est désolée, madame,*' murmured Ernestine from the stool beside the fireplace. '*La poésie.*'

Eugénie de Briand pulled Dell closer to herself and her fingers searched for Dell's face. They touched Dell's cheek lightly and suddenly Dell found her well of pent-up emotions overflowing.

'The poetry—of course! For you the memories are still too near, too painful. How thoughtless of me!'

How ironic! That this older woman, herself so keenly hurt by the loss of a loved one, should be trying to comfort her for all the wrong reasons ... Dell found herself kneeling, head in Eugénie de Briand's lap, sobs racking her body and a terrible sense of her own loss engulfing her.

Vaguely she heard Madame de Briand murmur a directive to Ernestine. Ernestine moved silently across the room. There was a clink of glass; something was handed to Madame de Briand, and then came the sound of Ernestine's feet padding away to the door.

When Dell finally raised her head, Ernestine had left the room. Eugénie de Brand was holding a glass of brandy. 'Take this, my dear. It will help restore you.'

'Th-thank you.' Dell took the glass gratefully and swallowed some of the liquid. It coursed like fire down her throat, at once searing and soothing.

She looked at Madame de Briand through red-rimmed eyes and was startled to see the ravages of time that showed in the older woman's face. Absurd, thought Dell, two women whom fate had brought to-gether for whatever bizarre reasons, weeping together for the might-have-been, for totally different might-have-beens.

'Please,' she choked, 'I'll be all right——'

'Of course,' soothed the older woman. 'Time heals even the scars of the soul. And perhaps, in time, one can remember the beauty and forget the pain.' She fingered the book of verse that lay now on her lap. 'Nothing, nothing can destroy the beauty, for either of us.'

Dell felt her soul shrivel with the weight of unspoken words, words that perhaps could never be spoken.

'You are sorrowing now,' continued Eugénie de Briand, 'and I do not deny that I too am sorrowing . . . for a time. But I will always remember that Rhys found happiness in you, a measure of content.' There was a magnificent sadness in her seamed face, a pride that told of suffering and strength. 'I might wish only that you and Rhys had married. That he had left us a child of his body; a grandchild of my own flesh.' She sighed heavily.

'But surely . . .' it wrenched Dell to say it, but she wished fiercely to give comfort to the older woman: 'Surely there's time yet. Raoul . . .'

'Pah! Raoul will never marry. The women, they make it too easy for him to take what he wants, to give nothing in return.' She sighed heavily.

'He seems attached to—Noëlle Rossignol.' Dell whispered the words although they twisted a knife in her heart.

'That one! If he marries her, she will never give him children.' Madame de Briand's lips thinned into a re-lentless line and suddenly Dell realised: it was Raoul's mouth, softer and more feminine perhaps, but it could be just as cruel.

'But that is another matter.' Eugénie de Briand's face had softened again. 'It is you that must concern me now.'

'Please don't worry about me. I don't get upset like this very often, really. It just came over me. I—I think I was just tired.'

'Perhaps you have been too much immersed in your work. You must take more time to yourself, see more of the countryside——'

'I did enjoy seeing Le Puy,' Dell admitted, glad that the conversation had moved away from personal matters.

'Then you must see more while you are here. There is much to see—ruins, monasteries, castles. Our small château is but a poor shadow of what the Auvergne has to offer. And there is great art to be seen. You have not yet been to La Chaise Dieu?'

'No—my train passed through there, that's all.'

'There is a fine mural there. La Danse Macabre ... death, enticing the nobility and the peasants in a faded, magnificent procession. A splendid thing in reds and blacks that have grown dim with time, but no less powerful. I must get Raoul to take you there. It is not so far—a pleasant day's expedition.'

The dance of death. Dell felt a shiver touch her spine. It sounded like a morbid outing. And she had no desire to be thrust into Raoul's company for another day. The less she saw of him the better. 'I'm afraid I'm still busy with sorting through papers.'

'There is no hurry to finish. You know you are welcome here as long as you wish to stay. As I said, I consider you my daughter-in-law.'

'You're very kind,' murmured Dell awkwardly. 'But my uncle is anxious to publish as soon as possible. I simply couldn't take another whole day to go sight-seeing.'

'*Eh bien*, you must allow Raoul to take you at least for a short picnic—an hour or two, nothing more. There is a place not far from here—Le Lac de l'Homme Perdu.'

'That sounds rather ominous!' Dell let a short laugh escape from her lips. 'The lake of the lost man?'

'A place less threatening than its name!' Eugénie de Briand leaned forward and her face flickered with a surprisingly youthful excitement. 'Many is the time that I ... but never mind. It is a beautiful spot, in truth. Below the village of Saint-Just—it lies in a cup of land between Montperdu and the village. You have passed close by on the road to Saint-Just. It is a deep gully of land, unbridged as are so many crevasses in this region, so that the road must wind around it before reaching the village. And in the gully is a small volcanic lake—a place of great charm.'

'Then why such a forlorn name? It sounds quite forsaken, really, as though it must have been the scene of tragedy.'

'Only in legend. There is a local belief that once there was a town where the lake now stands, an ancient town, more ancient even than the time of the Romans. The legend tells that a woman—a *sorcière*—came from afar and fell in love with a man of the town. But he scorned her love. He was a huntsman and afraid of nothing, not even a witch. Instead he was enamoured of a girl of the town, an engaging young filly.'

'What happened?'

'The woman swore that he should never have his

love. And if he did, the town would perish. But he only laughed ... and nightfall found him entwined in the arms of his young girl. When he placed his lips to hers, the *sorcière* caused a great upheaval of the earth. The town sank, and a rush of water poured in to cover it, boiling and hissing with the seething heat of the volcano and the venomous wishes of the witch. When the water cooled it became a lake, and to this day men think they can see the vanished buildings of the town beneath the surface on a still day.'

'Can they?' asked Dell quite seriously.

Madame de Briand shrugged. 'Who knows? There are many interesting rock formations beneath the surface and it is a shallow lake. As you know, the volcanic rock takes many colours and it happens there is a reddish cast to the stone in that area, giving it a russet look, a tint reminiscent of the tiled roofs of Le Puy, or indeed of Saint-Just-sur-Haute. In any case it is qiute a beautiful spot for a picnic.'

'Perhaps I'll go there one day,' said Dell.

'You shall,' returned the other woman prophetically. 'Now ... can you call Ernestine to take me to my room? I am an old woman, and this has been a wearying day. For you too. I cannot use my bell,' she indicated a silken pull that lay across the arm of her chair, 'because it is too late. It will disturb the other servants.'

'I'll take you myself,' offered Dell.

'No—no.' Eugénie de Briand waved her away. 'Ernestine is accustomed to administering to my needs. When one is dependent upon a certain routine ...' Her voice trailed away.

'I'll fetch Ernestine.'

It was strange, thought Dell later, how the interlude with Eugénie de Briand had calmed her troubled emotions. She knew now that it had been brewing inside her for some time—a storm of feeling, gathering in the recesses of her mind as the clouds gather water from the land, growing into tumultuous thunderheads of emotion. Now that the storm had been unleashed, serenity and a kind of strength had been restored. She knew she would not cry again.

In the weeks that followed Noëlle Rossignol turned up several times at the château. Dell, assessing her own reactions with a depth of understanding she had not had on first meeting the beautiful widow, managed to steel herself to the woman's visits, and school herself to betray nothing at all of what she felt.

But Noëlle was nobody's fool and Dell sensed the woman's resentment of her installation at the château. Dell found it safer to retire quietly to her turret room as soon as Noëlle arrived: and indeed, she had been throwing herself into the task of sorting Rhys's manuscripts with such single-minded dedication that it appeared the job would soon be finished. Already she had collated the material in several categories—three piles of works that might constitute different volumes of verse to be published right away; a pile for possible future consideration; a pile of rejects. She had only to sort and file the rejects. Further editing would have to be done in England.

Raoul she had scarcely seen at all. No doubt Noëlle sought him out on the occasions when she arrived at the château: Dell, hidden in her turret retreat, could not be sure. No doubt Raoul also spent considerable time at the Rossignol manoir. There had been little evidence of him about the château, although several times Dell had noticed Ernestine taking his evening meal to the studio. Perhaps he had been throwing himself into the task of completing Noëlle's portrait. Possibly he wished to finish it in time for his impending show in Paris, although Dell knew that the other paintings had already been taken away. She had seen them, one day, being loaded into a large moving van, wrapped in plastic sheeting and carefully layered between heavy padded tarpaulins.

Resolutely she pushed the thoughts from her mind. That route led only to a quagmire of self-pity. Better to concentrate on finishing her own job as soon as possible.

One evening, she heard Noëlle's small white Peugeot purr into the driveway shortly before the dinner hour. Dell had just come downstairs, freshly bathed and changed from her day's work, and had accepted a pre-dinner cocktail from Ernestine while waiting for Madame de Briand. She could hardly escape now ... except, perhaps, to the inner courtyard.

She slipped through the doorway that led to the sheltered square. The evenings were still somewhat cool, and her sheer printed cotton voile, layered over pale cotton in a simple Empire style, was attractive enough but hardly warm. However, the roses, now in early bloom, were enough to compensate for the chill of the evening. Dell reached over to pluck a particularly beautiful white rosebud.

'Ouch!' A thorn jabbed her and drew blood. She moved the stem gingerly to her other hand and sucked the crimson drop that formed on one fingertip.

'So, the thorny Miss Everett meets her match,' came

the silkily amused voice from across the courtyard. Dell
turned. It was Noëlle, wearing a magnificent gown of
magenta taffeta and gliding across the paving stones
with a controlled smile on her perfect face. Like some
gorgeous, full-blown red rose, thought Dell ruefully,
feeling woefully inelegant in her simple cotton.

'If you're looking for Raoul ...' she began, carefully
deleting the venom from her voice.

'Raoul will find me,' Noëlle said confidently, letting
her fingers trail negligently across a dozen rosebuds.
'He always does.'

'Can I offer you a drink—while you're waiting? Or
will you and Raoul be going out ... ?'

'Didn't Raoul tell you?' Noëlle arched an eyebrow.
'I'm invited for dinner this evening. A visit with
Maman. Something that must be done on occasion.'

Dell clamped her lips to restrain the angry retort
that almost came. Something in Noëlle's voice made it
sound like an unpleasant obligation, and the implied
familiarity of her words ... ! Maman, was it now!

'But Raoul insists,' continued Noëlle, her fingernail
slivering into a petal very daintily, very precisely.
'Something of importance—he wished to speak with
me this evening.'

She looked rather smug and Dell spoke hastily, not
wishing to hear any more. 'How is the portrait coming
along?'

Noëlle shrugged. 'He has been working on it night
and day. A man possessed.'

Possessed! Yes, by this witch of a woman, with her
flawless full-blown beauty.

'You're very lucky.' Dell felt a tight smile stiffening
her face. 'To be painted by Saint-Just is an honour.'

'Is someone taking my name in vain?' Raoul's voice

cut smoothly across the courtyard and Dell felt her whole body go rigid.

'But of course, *mon cher*!' Noëlle turned towards the newcomer with a seductive rustle of taffeta. 'We have been flattering you outrageously! Your ears must have been—how do you say it?—flaming!'

'Burning,' muttered Dell indelicately, possibly referring to her own emotions, but Noëlle ignored the interruption and moved smoothly towards Raoul, her gown whispering messages of soft nights and willing arms.

Raoul leaned over and deposited a perfunctory kiss on the proffered cheek. No doubt hampered by my presence, thought Dell achingly, and turned away towards the sliding door that led into the salon.

'What?' Raoul lifted an eyebrow. 'She escapes like a wraith of the night, the moment I put in an appearance? I assure you I'm hardly flattered by that.'

'It's getting quite chilly.' Dell hugged her shoulders coltishly, and indeed, she could feel the goose flesh rising over her skin.

'But then your dress is, how do you say it? a little nothing.' A small laugh from Noëlle, like a shivering of tinsel ... 'so sweet, but little warmth.'

'It *is* cool out here.' Raoul spoke, and Dell heard his footsteps nearing her across the flagstones. A moment later something dark and heavy dropped over her shoulders. It was his black silk dinner jacket, still warm from the masculine heat of his body. She squeezed her eyelids for a moment. This was as close as he had come to touching her since that day in Le Puy.

'Perhaps we should all go in.' Noëlle's voice betrayed a suggestion of something ... impatience, perhaps?

'Good idea.' Raoul moved ahead to open the door.

'I need a drink—you too, Noëlle.'

Once inside, Dell relinquished the jacket, laying it scrupulously over the back of a chair to avoid any possibility of chance contact with Raoul's hands, should he come to remove it from her. She watched him covertly as he mixed drinks for himself and Noëlle. The jacket still lay over the chair, and the silky cotton of his shirt revealed the breadth of his shoulders, the sinuous strength of his arms. The shirt was an ice blue, so pale as to appear almost white. An immaculate edging of fine eyelet embroidery ran down the front. His trousers, lean and black, betrayed the expert line and fit of the finest hand-stitched tailoring. Yet none of this was the Raoul she loved—not this civilised veneer, thinly laid over a creature of savage emotion. He was lean and dear and handsome and she loved him, but the Raoul she loved best wore a faded shirt and worn trousers.

'Raoul, that tailor of yours is simply superb!' Noëlle picked up the abandoned jacket and carried it across the room to Raoul. 'You must have him do more of your wardrobe in future ... perhaps some decent work clothes, even.'

Dell tried to suppress a small hysterical ripple of mirth. So her mind and Noëlle's had been working along the same channels! even if they were headed in different directions.

Raoul gave a glance in Dell's direction. 'Did you say something?' he asked.

'N-no,' she jerked the word out, trying hard to straighten her face. 'Just a cough, that's all.' As if in proof she put her hand up to cover her mouth. 'H-h-hem!'

'You did get a chill out there. Or perhaps working

in the tower,' he said, taking her glass to provide a re-fill. He spoke easily. 'Perhaps you'd like my jacket back again.'

'I'm quite warm now, thank you.' Control had re-turned and she returned his look levelly.

'Dell is not a child, Raoul,' Noëlle's voice held an edge of annoyance, 'to be bundled up and tucked into bed every time she sneezes.' She let her pliant white fingers trail down the shoulder of Raoul's jacket.

'I wonder,' he murmured, but he turned away as if in answer to Noëlle's soft urgings and Dell felt vaguely disappointed. Well, Raoul was old enough to take care of himself.

Noëlle had him by the arm now and was leading him away, towards the paintings on the wall. She looked up at Raoul archly, under lashes too thick to be true. 'And where will you hang your new portrait, Raoul, *mon cher*?'

Raoul looked at the wall consideringly before he answered: 'Not on this wall.'

Noëlle looked somewhat crestfallen. 'You are not—pleased with how the work progresses?'

'On the contrary,' returned Raoul smoothly, 'I think it's the best thing I've ever done.'

'Then you will be taking it to Paris for the show? When do you leave? Three, four days?'

'Yes. But I won't be taking this picture. I plan to hang it in my own suite of rooms, upstairs.'

'Ah!' Noëlle's voice was velvety with satisfaction. 'A place of honour, indeed. But do you not think the sub-ject might be pleased to let the work be seen, ad-mired——?'

'I prefer to keep it for my—my private delectation.'

'But ...' Noëlle pouted prettily and finished with a husky laugh: 'surely a mere portrait is second best to ...' she left the words hanging breathlessly in the air, and Dell mentally finished it for her. Second best to the real thing, second best to Noëlle Rossignol.

Dell pulled herself back into the recess of the wing chair as though it afforded some kind of protective colouration. It was almost as though they had forgotten she was here.

Raoul was sauntering back to the fireplace now. He hadn't answered Noëlle, but there was a half-smile on his face, and Noëlle glided behind him, her gown whispering echoes of triumph.

Dell pulled her eyes away and fixed them on the white-knuckled hands that clasped each other in her lap as though each had no other friend in the world. She had the strangest sensation that Raoul's eyes were boring into her, but when she looked up again he was staring into the fireplace.

'So you are fond of the portrait,' Noëlle continued after she had settled herself into a chair. 'I am—flattered.'

'Don't be,' Raoul said carelessly, no more tactful than usual. 'Wait until you've seen the portrait. You might be disappointed.'

'If you are pleased, Raoul, so will I be.' Noëlle smoothed the gleaming coil of hair that lay low on the nape of her shapely neck. 'But when will the unveiling take place? One is breathless with expectation.'

'Curiosity, my dear cat!' laughed Raoul. 'I never let anyone see portraits in progress.' Not strictly true, thought Dell. *I* saw it in progress.

Noëlle pretended a pout. 'But, *chéri* ...'

'No exceptions.' Raoul was firm. 'When I am painting it is as if the character unfolds before me on canvas. The canvas tells me things even the eye cannot see. To paint is a process of discovery.'

'A joyful process, one hopes.'

'Joyful—and painful. Discovering the beauty of a person often consists of stripping away a layer of untruths.'

'You mean like the series of portraits you did of Auvergnat peasant women?' Noëlle tilted an incredulous eyebrow. 'How you could find beauty in the person of that cook of yours . . .'

'Marie-Ange has a kind of beauty, a pride.' Raoul drained his glass and set it down on the table. Dell, remembering the rare smile that had transfigured Marie-Ange's homely face once before, silently agreed with him.

'Well, I call it genius on your part, Raoul, pure genius. One hopes you don't have to work so hard to find the beauty in your current subject.' Noëlle batted her eyelashes softly. The woman was really too ghastly obvious, thought Dell. She should have a black lace mantilla and a fan.

'I'm sure Raoul has no trouble at all, once he peels away the layers,' interjected Dell wickedly, and the other two turned to stare at her. Now I'm in for it, she thought, glancing at Noëlle's vituperative expression. Then at Raoul. A muscle was tugging at his jaw.

But she was saved. The door opened and Ernestine appeared, her hand tucked firmly beneath Madame de Briand's elbow.

CHAPTER NINE

THE evening had not gone too badly, all things considered. Noëlle had recovered her aplomb with great alacrity, and the moment of tension had passed. Noëlle had in fact become extremely good-natured as the evening progressed, even charming towards Dell. Probably something to do with my announcement that the work in the turret room is nearly finished, thought Dell wryly.

Madame de Briand had appeared to be disturbed at the news. 'But Dell, *ma chérie*! One more week only ...? Surely you can stay longer. It is so little.'

Raoul, on the other hand, had maintained an enigmatic silence until the conversation turned to other matters.

Dell let a small sigh escape her lips as she turned back to the pile of papers on her desk. It was cool in the turret room this morning and she wore heavy wool slacks and a cardigan.

Whether to file under first lines or under titles or under subject ... the decision seemed remarkably hard to make this morning. She felt decidedly restless. Probably the thought of tying up all the loose ends, the worst part of any job. Or was it the knowledge that, a week from now, she would be leaving Montperdu never to return? She had grown to love the place, to love the frail autocratic woman who lived here, to love ... But it was no use thinking about Raoul.

Determinedly she pulled her mind back to the papers on the desk. If only Rhys's handwriting were easier to decipher, less scored with alterations and deletions. This was a particularly messy page, one of his last poems but not one of his best. Probably written during some particularly alcoholic interlude, she decided. Perhaps if she typed it out she could make sense of the chaos of words. She put a fresh sheet of paper into the typewriter and started to work.

She had become quite absorbed in the task when the knock came at the door. Probably Ernestine come to tell her it was past lunch time, she thought with a cluck of annoyance. Ernestine always found it impossible to believe that anyone could work through the lunch hour.

She pulled her heavy cable-knit cardigan close about her and moored its belt more securely before going to the door.

It was Raoul. She felt her entire body go rigid of its own volition. This was the first time he had come to the turret room since that day so long ago ... What could he be doing here today?

'May I come in?' A flicker of a sardonic smile played across the harsh planes of his face. He was dressed in his working clothes: white paint-spattered jeans and a rumpled shirt of faded blue cotton, long in the sleeve but open at the throat. Dell riveted her eyes on the tense line of his collarbone to avoid contact with his eyes, and felt her throat constrict.

'Ah ... of course.' She stood aside, ushering him into the room, letting her eyes follow the back of his legs as they sauntered across to the desk. She left the door open—it was no use inviting trouble—and followed him across the room. Then she stood very still and waited for him to speak, her body trembling with a little prayer that this would not be another of those emotional bloodbaths.

'The work is nearly finished?' His fingers shifted some of the papers on the desk.

'Yes.' Keep it simple, Dell: that way there's less chance of trouble.

'Good.' He turned from the desk, almost impatiently. The sooner to get rid of you, my dear Miss Everett, thought Dell.

A hand came from behind his back and for the first time she noticed that he held a small package. It was loosely wrapped in white tissue paper, and untied. He held it out to her. 'A peace offering.'

Dell's hand refused to reach out for the parcel. She felt rooted to the ground, scarcely daring to breathe. 'It—isn't necessary.' Her words seemed thick and strange, even to her own ears.

'Take it.' He gave the tissue paper a little shake, and held it closer to her. 'You've brought great comfort to my mother. It's my way of saying thank you.'

'I can't——' The words seemed to strangle out of her throat.

'But you can, and will.' A glint of humour put those rare golden flecks back into his lava-dark eyes. 'It won't fit *me*.' He placed the tissued wrappings on the desk. 'There, if you won't take it from my hands.'

Very slowly Dell reached out and took the parcel. The tissue paper fell away and floated to the floor with a soft rustle, and she held up the contents with a gasp of astonishment and pleasure. It was the blouse she had admired in Le Puy. Raoul must have bought it that day. It seemed so long ago.

'But, Raoul ...' she turned great grey eyes to his, and felt her lashes fall again at the glimpse of something strange and sensual there.

'Wear it tonight.' His voice held a soft command.

'I can't do that.' Dell, recovering, tried to put dignity in the reply.

'Why not?' The voice was veiled: velvet on steel.

'Because I can't accept it.' She thrust the blouse back on to the desk. 'You must take it back. Or give it to— someone else.'

'If you mean Noëlle, she can look after herself in the gift department.' I'll bet she can, thought Dell cynically. He added: 'Besides, it wouldn't fit her. It's meant for someone much skinnier.'

Thanks for the compliment, Dell reflected wryly without voicing the thought. Instead she said: 'I don't want it.'

'Then you will take it because *I* want it.' His voice was quietly insistent.

'No.'

'A farewell gesture only.'

'No.' She was beginning to feel trapped. Why did he have to make it sound like a command?

'Dell ...' he turned away from her, and his voice sounded strained. 'It's important to me, I can't tell you why.'

'No!'

'—Please.'

The word came stiffly to his lips, as if uttered with great difficulty. Dell looked at the tense set of his shoulders. It was curious how he reminded her of her uncle at times. A man with too much pride to beg.

'All right, I—I'll accept it.' The words had spilled out before she had a chance to think them through.

Raoul was silent for a moment, but his shoulders eased perceptibly, and then he turned back to face her. 'Promise, then. Wear it tonight.'

'I promise.' She laughed rather nervously. 'Although I can't see why it's so important.'

'I'll tell you tomorrow.' A smile crinkled the corners of his eyes and for a moment he looked quite human. Dell felt a small wrench at her heart, a hollowness in the pit of her stomach. Raoul sank into the swivel chair and tilted it backwards, satisfaction apparent in the nonchalant way he laced his fingers behind his head.

'So. The competent Miss Everett has untangled the Gordian knot. The work looks very well organised.' He nodded towards the neatly labelled manuscript-size envelopes stacked on a corner of the desk, each containing its own assortment of poems.

'Those are ready to go.' Dell gestured at the pile. 'You can look them over any time. I think you said you wanted to see anything that was to be released.'

'I've changed my mind.' His voice was lazy. He indicated the pile of papers still loose on the desk. 'How about these?'

'Rejects. I didn't think they were worth publishing, at least not right now. They're for sorting and filing.'

'Hmmm.' He picked one up, scanned it, and tossed it carelessly on the desk. 'I think you're right.'

'Some of them I'm not sure about; there are so many corrections.'

'Like this?' From beside the typewriter he picked up the poem Dell had been working on: Rhys' handwriting, heavily scored, with numerous marginal corrections.

'I've been trying to make head or tail of that one. I've just finished it.'

'I see.' He leaned over towards the typewriter and rolled up the carriage to read the finished words. 'No, not—his best.' He flashed a curious, considering look at her; an appraisal that made her feel as though he had peeled away yet another layer of her consciousness.

Then he swivelled the chair away from the typewriter and unfolded his limbs, a lithe mountain-cat movement that stirred a tremulous sense of awareness within her, although she refused to let it show in the schooled passionlessness of her expression. He moved to the door. 'Till later, then. Remember your promise.'

After he had left, Dell found it impossible to return to the musty papers. Rhys' scribblings no longer seemed to make any sort of sense at all. In any case, it really was past lunch time. Ernestine would be clucking over the uneaten food like a mother hen. Perhaps, too, it would be a good idea to take the afternoon for personal matters—letters to be written to her aunt and uncle; a few clothes to be washed and mended; perhaps a nap and a leisurely soak in the tub ... Yes, she had earned an afternoon off.

Deciding to tidy up for the next day, she pulled the finished poem from the typewriter. A line caught her eye: '... behind the midnight curtain of her coal-black hair ...' She had scarcely paid attention earlier; she had been too caught up in the problem of deciphering the words. Coal-black, midnight ... the colour of Sally's hair. A small point, perhaps, but she wondered if

Raoul would have noticed the discrepancy.

But then even if he had, it would do nothing to improve his opinion of her. He thought of her, and probably would always think of her, as an immoral woman, the person who was responsible for his half-brother's death. Dell sighed, and turned to leave the room with a heavy heart. She looked back to check that she had forgotten nothing.

The blouse—of course. And she *had* promised. She returned to the desk and picked up the garment, not without a tremor of the fingers.

It was later, much later, when she tried the blouse on. The afternoon's unaccustomed sleep had left her with a delightful lethargy of the limbs, a sort of disembodied slow-motion sensation that nothing seemed to dispel—not the long leisurely soaking in a fragrant bath, not even the shampoo, nor the brushing of her hair to a burnished glow. It was as though her body were sleeping, waiting to be wakened ... Dell pushed the thought aside and returned to the business of dressing.

The blouse fitted as though it had been made for her. She peered into the mirror, eyes still heavy-lidded. She supposed she should feel self-conscious about the swell of breast that was half-revealed by the plunging bodice, but somehow in her state of languor she failed to be disturbed.

She had chosen a simple velvet skirt of a russet brown to complement the pale lace of the blouse. Its waistband rose several inches, high enough to meet the deep vee of the neck. She had plucked a rose earlier this afternoon, a pale unusual coppery pink that blended beautifully with the tone of the skirt, and she tucked it now into the rise of her waistband. She had no jewellery that would do justice to the exquisitely heavy hand-made lace, and rather than wear costume jewellery she had decided to do without. She darkened her eyebrows lightly and traced the outline of her lips with a colour that exactly matched the flower at her waist. A last fleeting glance in the mirror ... she couldn't decide whether she looked seductive or demure. But what did it matter anyway?

It was later than usual when she arrived in the salon. Madame de Briand was already waiting, ensconced in her favourite wing chair; and Raoul—Dell's heart did a minor flip-flop—stood by the fireplace with indolent grace, darkly handsome in his midnight blue dinner suit. His eyebrows winged upwards at the sight of Dell, and a fleeting look of satisfaction crossed his face.

'Tonight, an English rose,' he murmured, and Dell found the colour rising to her cheeks. Suddenly she felt totally conscious of the revealing neckline that had seemed so unimportant in the privacy of her room. A smile lingered on Raoul's face. 'You remembered your promise.'

Madame de Briand pricked her ears, straightening in her chair and straining her head towards Dell almost as though she were trying to see through the veil of sightlessness. 'What is this? What promise?'

Raoul laughed easily. 'Dell promised to wear a blouse that she found in Le Puy. A champagne lace, very pretty. She looks like an English tea rose.'

'Humph! Champagne. Not the right colour for a tea rose,' remarked Madame de Briand.

'You should see the blush that goes with it,' he observed.

'Raoul, stop making Delilah feel self-conscious, and pour her a drink,' ordered Madame de Briand. 'And I will have another Perrier, while you're about it.'

Through the drinks and the dinner that followed, Dell's acute sense of embarrassment eased. At first she sat rigidly uncomfortable and ramrod-stiff, afraid to bend forward in case the neckline of her blouse revealed more than it should; even more afraid to look in Raoul's direction in case her eyes revealed the turbulent emotions that warred within her. Madame de Briand spent much of the meal urging that Dell should reconsider her decision to leave. Dell scarcely dared to respond, lest by her answers she should betray her own unwillingness to go. If only it were Raoul who wished her to stay! But if the idea of Dell's departure gave him more than a twinge of unease, he managed to hide it well. If anything, he seemed more expansive than usual —happier and more relaxed, she thought, than she had seen him since the day in Le Puy. Perhaps he felt he could afford to be generous in view of her near departure. Or perhaps he was buoyed up by the approach of his opening in Paris. Several times she could feel his eyes seeking hers, smoky in the soft light of the candles, but she refused to return their gaze. Nevertheless, the meal and the wine and Raoul's apparent good humour served their purpose, and she found herself gradually becoming less ill at ease as the evening progressed.

'By the way, Raoul, Ernestine tells me that Noëlle was here again today.' They were returning to the salon now: Eugénie de Briand with her arm enlaced in Raoul's, picking her way across the dark Bokhara rug. Dell followed a pace behind.

'Oh?' Raoul settled his mother in her favourite chair

and ambled over to the drinks cabinet, apparently unconcerned. 'A liqueur, Maman?'

'Thank you, no.' Madame de Briand paused while Raoul poured two glasses of brandy and delivered one to Dell. She accepted it gratefully, wondering how he had sensed her preference without asking.

'I believe Noëlle left you a note,' continued Eugénie de Briand once Raoul had returned to stand at the fireplace. 'But perhaps Ernestine has already given it to you.'

'No,' he said. 'Ernestine has orders not to disturb me, except to bring meals, when I'm at work in the studio. And I haven't seen her since I stopped working. Perhaps she left it in the study.'

'Then——' the frail woman pulled at the silken bellpull that hung within reach over one arm of her chair, 'then Ernestine shall bring it to you here.'

In moments Ernestine bustled into the room, solicitous and efficient as ever, apron starched to a papery crispness.

'Madame?'

'Yes, Ernestine. The note from Madame Rossignol, *s'il vous plaît*. And also, the blue velvet case I laid upon my chiffonière this afternoon. You remember.'

'*Mais oui, madame,*' and Ernestine rustled out of the room.

'Would you—would you mind very much if I said goodnight now?' Dell turned to Madame de Briand after Ernestine had left. Her brandy sat on the table beside her, untouched after all. Somehow, the evening had turned sour. 'I'm really rather tired.'

'Please stay.' Eugénie de Briand's response was an order, gently phrased and softly spoken, but a command nonetheless. She laid her hands calmly against the moiré silk of her dress, a dark plum colour with fine ruching on the bodice. 'Now, Raoul, what can that Rossignol woman have to say that she could not have said last night? She stayed long enough after Dell and I went off to bed. Tell me, Dell, do you not think Raoul is entirely too involved with this woman Rossignol?'

But just then Ernestine appeared at the door and Dell was spared the necessity of answering. Raoul strode across the room and accepted from her a large blue velvet jewel case, and a small mauve envelope—perfumed, no doubt, Dell thought. Ernestine bowed out; Raoul returned to the fireplace and handed the jewel case to his mother before opening the note.

A ghost of a smile flitted across his face as he perused its contents, and Dell, unable to bear this visible proof of his attachment to Noëlle Rossignol, veiled her eyes to stare at the slender white hands that lay in her lap. She could hear the rustle of notepaper being put away —no doubt close to his heart—and, somewhere in the back of her consciousness, the snap of the jewel case being opened.

'Tell me, Delilah,' Madame de Briand's voice broke into the moment of silence, 'are you wearing any jewellery? Ernestine tells me you have very little.'

'O-only a flower,' stuttered Dell, suddenly dreading what she knew was to come.

'Then, my dear, take these. They were given to me by Rhys' father, Emlyn Morgan.' She pulled a heavy triple rope of pearls from the case. They were large, lustrous, very long, perfectly matched, glowing with the depth of creamy splendour that only genuine pearls could achieve. They were as beautiful as Dell had known they would be ever since she had first seen them in the portrait of Eugénie de Briand. The older woman spoke again: 'I can no longer enjoy their lustre, and the style is too youthful, too heavy for my old body.'

'But I can't take them!' Dell was aghast. The second present in one day—and these, their value exceeding anything she had ever dreamed of, should become family heirlooms. She couldn't possibly take them under false pretences. It was bad enough that Eugénie de Briand had come to consider her one of the family, but to take advantage of the lie she was living ... ! It was impossible.

'You can, and you will.' The aged velvet voice took on an authoritative ring. Weren't those the words Raoul had used, earlier today? But this time, nothing would make her give in.

'No, please, no!' she countered, miserably.

'Raoul, Dell is going to be difficult. Take the pearls and put them on her,' demanded Eugénie de Briand, holding the heavy rope towards her son.

'*Avec plaisir.*' The words made Raoul seem very foreign and very frightening, somehow, and Dell sat frozen with dismay as he retrieved the pearls from Madame de Briand and walked over, circling the chair until he was behind Dell's back.

Slowly his hands moved the rope around her neck and Dell felt as though her heart, her pulse, her very breath had been suspended in a state of shock.

She could feel his hands brushing lightly on the back of her neck as he fastened the clasp. Then the small hairs of her nape rising, straining as though to meet his fingers ... then the weight of the pearls plummeting between her breasts, a cold heavy startling sensation. She sat rigidly, her hands refusing to move, refusing to fight the temptation to let things take their course. In the swimming background of her vision she could see the sightless face of Madame de Briand, wearing a small secret smile of satisfaction; but her total consciousness, her entire being seemed to be swallowed up in the warmth of Raoul's fingers and the cold sensuous weight of the pearls.

Then, still paralysed with a sense of unreality, she felt his hands travel over her shoulders ... a hand reached down, and pulled the rose from its pinnings at her waist. Then the hand trailed upward, a shivering touch, a soft shock wave of sensation. She could feel his fingers lingering over the sweet rise of her breast, insinuating themselves against the firmness of flesh beneath the verges of lace, stealing over with an intimacy that she seemed powerless to prevent, to brush the rise of nipple. His breath was a gentle warmth against the soft shell of her ear and Dell felt her senses reeling, pulling her into a vortex of emotion, a whirlpool of feeling, down, down, down ...

'Well, Raoul? How do they suit?' It was like a dash of cold water.

Dell leaped to her feet, pulses pounding now, brain thundering with the sense of her own impropriety, limbs trembling with a terrible weakness.

'I can't take them! They don't belong to me!'

'They do now,' soothed Madame de Briand, puzzlement creasing her forehead. 'I have just given them to you. Rhys would have wanted you to have them.'

'No.' Dell's voice ached with the effort of her words. 'He——'

'They would have been yours, on your wedding day.'

'But——'

'Keep them, my child, if not for Rhys' sake, then for mine.'

'But Rhys didn't—love me.' Dell heard her own voice as if in a dream, distant, unreal. 'It wasn't—the way you think.'

For a moment Madame de Briand waited in silence, her brow still seamed with perplexity. Then she spoke, very slowly, as if feeling her way through a vast abyss of understanding. 'Yet—for the love you bore him.'

'I didn't love Rhys. I never loved Rhys!' The words flooded out now, like a dam burst loose. 'We never, never intended to marry. It was just a—pretence, something to keep Rhys out of trouble with—with all those adoring females who used to throw themselves at him!' Dell sucked in her breath at the enormity of what she had said, and finished lamely: 'That's all.'

'But the poetry. The book,' Madame de Briand protested. 'Surely . . .'

'It wasn't me, don't you see? It was about a lot of— other women. It never was *one* woman with Rhys.'

'But it was you who meant most to him, surely. After all, *To Delilah*. . .'

'No.' Dell's tongue felt as if cloven to her palate. She desperately wished she could say something to wipe away the terrible look on Eugénie de Briand's face, to turn back the clock. But now it was too late. The damage was done, and truth, a stern master, drove her on. 'It wasn't me, it never could have been me. Rhys loved nobody—and everybody. Nothing he wrote, nothing, had anything at all to do with me. I was just a—business arrangement.'

'Dell! What are you saying!' Madame de Briand had gone totally white now, her face glazed with disbelief.

'I'm saying I—I'm sorry, I can't take the pearls.' Dell fumbled with the catch at the back of her neck, but it resisted her fingers. Finally she gave up the effort and buried her face in her hands. 'It was all a terrible mistake.'

'Mistake? And all this time you have allowed me to believe ...' the words curdled in Eugénie de Briand's throat, and her face crumpled visibly, like a thin tissue paper that has been used too often.

'It seemed—I thought it was kinder.' Dell had the sensation of being trapped, and looked around for Raoul with an anguished appeal in her eyes. He stood, panther-like, tense with watchfulness, still leaning against the chair where Dell had been sitting moments before. His eyes were grave now, the brow knitted with concern, but he wasn't looking at her. He was looking at his mother. No use expecting any help from that quarter.

Dell swallowed painfully, and turned again to Madame de Briand. 'I—I almost wish it had been true.' Then, because the time for lies had past: 'No, I don't mean that, not as far as Rhys is concerned, anyway. But for your sake.'

'For *my* sake?' Eugénie de Briand had pulled herself forward in the chair, dark and rageful and magnificent in her plum-coloured silks. Her mouth had that look of Raoul's again, a cruel vengeful line. It was as though the strength had flowed back into her ravaged body with a surge of hatred. 'All this pretence for *my* sake? You have deceived me, child. And

I do not like to be deceived.'

'I——'

'You led me to believe you were engaged to Rhys.'

'I was! The engagement was real enough. But it was purely a business arrangement, to protect Rhys.'

'You let me believe you loved him.'

'I didn't actually say so.'

'You did not deny it.'

Dell studied her fingers remorsefully. 'The deception was never intended to hurt—anyone.'

Eugénie de Briand's face became a rigid mask of itself, carved in unrelenting stone. She sank slowly back into her chair. 'A deception, nevertheless. There is no more to be said.'

Dell could not deny it, so she turned in shaky silence towards the door, hoping her feet would not betray her now. Raoul remained standing behind the chair, watching her with inscrutable eyes as she walked unsteadily from the room. Only after she had reached the hall did she realise that one hand was clasped fiercely around the triple rope of pearls.

Pearls for unhappiness, she thought; pearls that lay against her heart like stones, as heavy and cold and accusing as the face of Madame de Briand.

CHAPTER TEN

RAOUL caught up with her in the dim large hall of the château, barring her exit up the stairs.

'Dell——' he started, but she turned on him like a wounded animal at bay, eyes desperate and shoulders trembling with the pent-up emotions that had been building within her through the preceding nightmarish half hour.

'You!' She choked the word at him. 'It's all your fault!' That this was patently untrue, she was too wrought up to sort out in her mind.

He lifted his eyebrows in mild surprise. 'Really?'

'Yes, really! If you hadn't made me wear this ... this ...' She gestured angrily at the blouse.

'Very becoming. But it has nothing to do with what happened tonight.'

'No? If it hadn't—if you hadn't—touched me——' Suddenly she felt confused.

'You would nevertheless have refused the pearls.' His eyes were smoky and unreadable in the half-light.

'I can't explain.' She made as if to turn away, but his hand caught at her arm, insistently.

'Don't deceive yourself, Dell,' he said softly.

'It's you who deceived me.' Her voice was low, scarcely louder than a whisper. 'Extracting that ridiculous promise to wear the blouse. And all for no earthly reason except ..., except ...'

'You have no idea what my reasons were,' he interjected calmly.

151

She looked at him then, a bitter unforgiving look that pitched her eyes in battle against his. Suddenly he dropped his hand, and Dell realised how deep had been the pressure of his fingers against the flesh of her arm. His eyes frosted over. Without another word he turned, and stalked out the front door.

Now, in her bedroom, she could almost hear the heavy clang of it still ringing in her ears.

She drew the hateful blouse over her head and threw it into a corner of the armoire. Why had Raoul insisted that she wear the thing anyway? Perversely she felt that, had it not been for the awful chaos of her senses aroused by Raoul's touch, she would have found a kinder way to refuse the pearls. Or perhaps she would have accepted them, as graciously as possible: then quietly left them behind, on her departure from Montperdu next week. They lay, now, coiled opulently on her dressing table, pale, perfect, reproachful. And there they would stay.

Dry-eyed and almost without reaching a conscious decision, Dell found herself pulling a suitcase from the large armoire. There was nothing left for her here. Things had been said between herself and Eugénie de Briand that could never be unsaid. She had brought only unhappiness to the older woman, a woman whom, moreover, she respected and had grown to love. Her presence, if she remained, would only serve to remind Madame de Briand of a son best forgotten. Or at least, best held in memory for the beauty of his words, if not his life.

But even more pressing was the need to escape from Raoul. She did not feel she could face him, again, ever, remembering how he had touched her. It was an impossible situation—oh, not for Raoul, perhaps, but certainly for herself. What had possessed her to sit in a state of paralysis while he removed the rose, touched her so insinuatingly ... the very memory of it sent cold fingers of fire over her body.

And for Raoul? He had told her, long ago, that she would not be forgiven if she brought more pain to his mother's life. And that she had assuredly done. Her departure could only cause relief. Certainly it would be no more than a ripple on the surface of his existence. Probably with the imminence of his show in Paris he would hardly even take note of her leaving.

She would be letting her uncle down, of course; and she felt a heaviness of heart to think she would be returning to England without the manuscripts he awaited so eagerly. But it couldn't be helped. She wouldn't dare remove Rhys' things without permission. But at least most of the initial work had been done; and if permission could be obtained by her uncle at a later date, the envelopes could follow by mail. Someone else would have to sort and file the rejects.

Dell slipped into a pair of slacks and a shaggy sweater. The night was still ahead and there were plans to be made. First, an outfit for travelling tomorrow: she laid out a simple short-sleeved cotton shirt dress of navy blue. It would be cool and practical for the journey, as the days were now quite warm. Then a pair of high-heeled sandals, pantyhose she laid these out to wear in the morning, and packed all her other clothes into the suitcases. She would take only one of these with her. Her other baggage would have to follow; Ernestine could have it shipped to her.

Dell lay down on the bed and waited, her dry eyes

staring at the moulded ceiling. This night would be a long vigil for her if she were to be away early; and she dared not sleep now. There was still the problem of getting her one suitcase into the car without arousing the suspicions of anyone else in the household: something that would have to be done in the still shank of the night, while the others slept.

Her mind raced ahead, busy with plans. She'd take the old Renault—she'd think of an excuse—and leave it at the station in Saint-Just-sur-Haute. Gaspard or Raoul could bring it back from there, surely a small price to pay for being rid of their unwelcome visitor.

At three o'clock in the morning she slipped silently out the door of her room and tiptoed down the hall with the suitcase, feeling her way in the dark. When she reached the main hall, passage became easier. A thin shaft of moonlight seeped through the large window in the stairway, lending a ghostly pallor to the entrance-way. The ancient château slept like a shadow out of time, a memory of mediaeval strongholds in the night.

She held her breath as the front door creaked open. Outside visibility was a little easier, for it was a clear cloudless night, soft and still, laying an almost phosphorescent magic over the stone façade of the château. She padded noiselessly across the smooth cobblestones, glad of the soft-soled slippers she had worn. The Renault was parked, she knew, in the small garage beyond the stables—the studio, Raoul's studio.

Fortunately the door of the garage was open, and Dell eased her way through the opening.

It was very dark inside the building, and she almost stumbled over something large and cold and heavy. She put her suitcase down and groped in the blackness.

No, this was Raoul's Porsche. Again she tried, moving cautiously through the yawning emptiness of vision. This time she had more luck. It was the Renault—thank heaven, unlocked.

She placed her suitcase on the floor in the rear seat. Feeling about, she found a mound of something soft; it felt like the old afghan she had seen in the back seat on the night of her arrival. She pulled it over the suitcase, hoping the lump would not appear too suspicious by daylight.

There, she was done. She didn't dare slam the car door. Instead she pushed it gently until it caught lightly against the frame of the car. If her luck held, perhaps no one would notice.

In moments she had found her way back to the narrow strip of light that defined the door of the garage, and tiptoed out on the cobbles of the courtyard, scarcely daring to breathe. Just beyond the door to the stable her foot caught on something hard. Damn! One of the hitching posts. A dull metallic clang resounded in the night and she caught her breath, darting into the shadows at the side of the building.

She could feel her heart hammering furiously. Would anyone have heard the noise—Ernestine perhaps, with her sharp ears?

A door clicked open. It was Raoul, in the studio! Brilliance poured from inside the studio door, laying a strong pattern of light and shadow over the cobbled stones of the courtyard. Dell shrank back into the protective darkness.

He emerged from the studio and Dell could see his strong frame silhouetted in the light from the doorway. He still held a paintbrush in one hand. Obviously he had been interrupted in his work on Noëlle's portrait. He looked about nonchalantly, one thumb hooked into the pocket of his trousers ... the Raoul she loved, and would never see again.

Then, finally satisfied that nothing was amiss, he shrugged and retreated back into the stable. The door closed behind him with a soft click and for a moment Dell squeezed her eyes, adjusting them to the softer evanescence of the moonlight. It was several minutes before she dared to attempt the trip back to her room.

Long before the dawn broke over the mountains, she was dressed and ready to go. Now for the matter of requesting the use of the car. Would she say she was going on a picnic? No, she was hardly dressed for that. Then she remembered the conversation she had had with Madame de Briand several weeks ago. The mural at La Chaise Dieu, la Danse Macabre ... surely she could announce that she planned a day of sightseeing in that town! Eugénie de Briand had said it would be a day's expedition. That should allay everyone's suspicions at least until nightfall, by which time she would be well on the way to Paris.

She considered the plan carefully in her mind, turning it this way and that to see if there were any loopholes. As she didn't know what time the northbound train passed through Saint-Just-sur-Haute, it would be necessary to get to the station as soon as possible. She'd have an early breakfast—breakfast was always early here, in any case; get the car keys from Gaspard; and be on her way. Raoul would undoubtedly sleep late after his long night of work. And Madame de Briand never rose at that time of the morning.

Yes, it was an admirable plan. Should she leave a

note, explaining where the car could be found? She decided no. Saint-Just-sur-Haute was a small village, and news of the Renault's presence, parked in the vicinity of the station, would filter back soon enough. And there was always the chance that a note would be found by Héloise too early in the day, while she was on her round of cleaning, and given to Raoul or Madame de Briand before Dell had a chance to make good her departure.

Ernestine looked mildly surprised when Dell arrived for breakfast somewhat earlier than usual. She looked suspiciously at her eyes—no doubt she had heard of the events of last night—and Dell was glad that she had not wept. Ernestine was too observant by half.

'Mademoiselle 'as not slept well?' she asked solicitously. 'You 'ave risen early. The breakfast will be a few moments.'

'I slept perfectly well, Ernestine.' Dell tried to sound cheerful and hoped that the shadows of her eyes didn't give her statement the lie. 'I'm up early because I've planned a day of sightseeing. Madame de Briand told me I should see the mural at La Chaise Dieu. I've been working quite hard and today is Saturday, so ...' She nearly bit her tongue. It wouldn't do to protest too much. She would have to be careful with Ernestine.

Ernestine looked surprised. 'Bue——' then she stopped, and compressed her lips into a thin line. 'Monsieur Raoul, 'e will not like it.'

'Monsieur Raoul is not my keeper. I'm perfectly capable of finding my way about, and I can handle the Renault very nicely.'

'Monsieur Raoul, 'e will be angry.' Ernestine was adamant.

'Then I'll have to deal with him later, won't I, Ernestine? Just let me have my breakfast now, anything simple. Monsieur Raoul can hardly hold you responsible for my actions.'

'Monsieur Raoul——' stated Ernestine stubbornly.

'Madame de Briand told me I could use the car any time I wished,' interrupted Dell firmly.

'But surely, after last night——' Ernestine began.

'What about last night?' said Dell coolly, looking Ernestine squarely in the eye and daring her to pursue the matter.

Ernestine withdrew her gaze and turned towards the kitchen. 'I will get breakfast for Mademoiselle,' she said deferentially, but with a trace of defiance. As Ernestine retreated to the kitchen Dell could hear the woman still mumbling to herself, her head wagging disapprovingly, 'Monsieur Raoul, 'e will not like it.'

Dell did her best to do justice to the rolls and coffee that appeared moments later, but eating was a distinct effort. Had it not been for the suspicious hovering of Ernestine, she would have passed the meal up entirely. But the coffee, black and almost bitter with strength, was welcome.

'Mademoiselle would like a lunch packed, per'aps? It is a long drive.' At last Ernestine had accepted the fact that Dell intended to make the trip, regardless of her remonstrances.

'No, thank you, Ernestine,' refused Dell, trying to keep her voice breezy. 'Surely there are places to eat in La Chaise Dieu? I'd like to sample some of the local restaurants.'

'As you wish, *mademoiselle*. But Marie-Ange has made a fine rabbit pâté ... and there is cold chicken.

It would take only a moment.'

Dell smiled warmly, appreciative of the woman's solicitude. 'You're very kind, Ernestine, but all I need is the car keys—and a road map. Can you tell me where to find Gaspard?'

'I will send him to you, *mademoiselle*. 'E is eating his breakfast in the kitchen.' She vanished through the door.

It took only moments to get the directions from Gaspard—directions she would never use, but it was part of the smoke screen necessary for her departure. Evidently Gaspard had not been out to the garage this morning, and had found nothing amiss. He bobbed his head obligingly and warned Dell to drive carefully; rain had been predicted and sometimes the roads were slippery and difficult, even washed out if the downpour were sufficient. And in the Auvergne, a downpour could be torrential.

'Don't worry, Gaspard,' she reassured him, 'I'll treat the car with kid gloves.'

'Keed gloves? *Je ne comprends pas*.' He looked puzzled.

'Never mind, Gaspard,' she laughed. 'I'll drive carefully, have no fear.'

'Ah! The car is—fix now,' he added, 'but it is old, *très vieux*. One hopes——'

'It will be perfectly all right, Gaspard. Don't worry. *Soyez tranquille*.'

Gaspard shrugged, and offered to bring the car to the front door. Dell agreed gratefully. It would save her the trip past the stable door. Raoul was probably in bed now, sound asleep—but what if he had continued to work through the night? A chance encounter would be more than she could bear right now.

The ignition caught easily enough, and the car shuddered into action. Dell allowed herself a last look at the château that had come to figure so prominently in her life. Today Montperdu looked grey and foreboding under a leaden sky. Perhaps the threatened rain would break soon. But by then she should be safely on her way to Paris, or at least quietly awaiting the train's arrival in the station at Saint-Just-sur-Haute.

The trip down the spiral of road brought its own memories, a painful procession of visions: Raoul, his hands gripping tensely on the wheel of his car; Raoul, laughing and carefree on the way to Le Puy; Raoul, a disembodied voice in the night, lashing out in fury at her on the way back from Noëlle Rossignol's *manoir* that same night.

Resolutely she tried to shut the memories from her mind. At the base of the mountain, where the road to Montperdu branched into the main road, she swung to the left, towards Saint-Just-sur-Haute. To the right lay the way to La Chaise Dieu. Perhaps, later, they would be searching for her in that direction.

A mile or so further along the road started to wind uphill again, rising towards the village, which was still several miles away by this circuitous route. The car was complaining now, an odd choking sound that caught at the motor like a stutter. Surely it wasn't low on petrol? Dell checked. No: the dial showed a full tank.

Then, suddenly, there was a total cessation of power, and ahead lay a steep hill. Damn! Dell geared down, pulled the choke out to its fullest, and pushed her foot against the accelerator. Nothing. Nothing! And the village of Saint-Just-sur-Haute was still six, maybe seven miles away. The car eased to a halt, stubbornly, and she applied the handbrake.

What was to be done? She had just passed the turn-off to Noëlle Rossignol's place, not a hundred yards further down the hill. But nothing, nothing could induce her to approach the woman for help. She had no option but to walk into Saint-Just, leaving the car where it was.

But then what if Raoul or Gaspard were out on the road later this morning? They would see the Renault and instantly know something was wrong. Perhaps if she backed the car up, left it in the twisting gravel road that led to the Rossignol *manoir*? But of course, Raoul might be taking that route too. Most likely he would be taking that route! The knowledge gave Dell a wrench.

Never mind. If she left the Renault where it was now, someone would be sure to see it and inform the de Briands. At least there was a chance it wouldn't be seen for a while—not till this afternoon at least—if she left it off the main road. And if it were on the way to Noëlle's home, Raoul would be sure to find it eventually, perhaps even this evening.

Slowly she released the handbrake and, craning over her shoulder, allowed the car to drift backwards down the road. Here came the cut-off into Noëlle's place ... she negotiated the bend carefully. Thank goodness the road still led downhill. Another hundred yards down the side road there was a thick clump of bushes, standing close to the ribbon of gravel. She steered the car in behind it and braked to a halt. The car was screened from the main road now, but perfectly visible from the tortuous lane that led down to Noëlle's house.

Satisfied, Dell applied the handbrake and breathed deeply. She left the keys dangling in the ignition and stepped out of the car, taking care not to snag her pantyhose on the nearby brambles.

Then she opened the back door and uncovered the hidden suitcase. What to do? It was too heavy to carry all the way to Saint-Just; she wouldn't even try. It would have to follow with the rest of her luggage, later on. But there were a few things she might need.

She opened the case and extracted the auburn-toned angora cardigan coat she had worn in Le Puy. It would stand her in good stead as a light covering, should she need it this evening. She would have preferred her red cardigan; it wasn't quite so heavy and would dry faster should she get caught in the rain. Then she remembered with annoyance that she hadn't seen it for some time. It must still be in Raoul's studio, abandoned that day so long ago, when she had retreated in such confusion. Well, it couldn't be helped now.

She pulled out an extra pair of pantyhose—they might come in handy. Then a toothbrush, toothpaste, a hairbrush. Her make-up kit, a simple affair, was already in her capacious handbag, along with her passport and other essentials of travel. Everything else would have to wait.

She started along the climb of road, cursing the high-heeled sandals that made walking something less than comfortable. It was uphill work and it was scarcely easier on the main road than it had been on the rough Rossignol lane.

When she reached the top of the rise, past where her car had first halted, she paused to consider. This way, it might be mid-afternoon before she reached Saint-Just. And it looked as if it might rain any moment now; the air was still and heavy with a sultry humidity. If only she could remove her shoes, it might speed the walking. But the gravel of the road was needle-sharp. Walking on its surface without protection would be ruinous to her tights—and to her feet. The frustration mounted within her. To be so near and yet so far! Saint-Just perched on the crest of the hill opposite, not more than two miles away in a straight line, but the road wound away to the right, only to return to the village after a circuitous route around the mountains.

Below lay a verdant valley, a gully really, that ran downwards on a gentle slope and then rose more steeply towards the village. Dell could feel her already-aching feet fairly itching to curl their toes into the soft green tendrils of grass.

At the bottom of the valley was a stand of trees, and beyond that lay outcroppings of russet rock. Dell thought she saw evidence of a narrow stream, too, but it looked quite negotiable. She squinted into the distance, her eyes searching for signs of a path to Saint-Just-sur-Haute. Yes, there seemed to be a ribbon of clearing between the bushes that grew on the far mountainside, below the village. It was steep, but not too steep ... surely she could save hours by walking through this pleasant treed gully.

The decision made, she walked to the far edge of the road and removed her sling sandals, dropping them into her handbag. Then, swiftly, she stripped off her pantyhose and stuffed them into the toe of one shoe. She'd always loved walking barefoot in the grass anyway.

The turf was cool and springy to her feet, still dewed with early-morning dampness. It was a relief from the almost oppressive heat that lay over the mountain—the air held motionless, it semed, by the close heavy cover of cloud. The sky really looked quite ominous now, and Dell hoped it wouldn't rain before she reached the station house. A half-hearted laugh escaped her. At least the dress was drip-dry!

She was almost at the bottom of the valley now. A thicket of trees lay ahead, oak and beech interspersed with dark coniferous species, and an icy rivulet trickled on a stony downward path to the floor of the gully. In the grassy distance Dell could see a huddle of brown cattle, sensing the coming storm and grouping together for protection.

Then, a blaze of late-blooming narcissi peeped out from behind a knoll of land and her spirits rose a notch. Life couldn't be all that bad!

She followed the winding stream through the thicket. Then the trees cleared, and to her astonishment she saw a small finger of lake stretching before her. It must have been hidden from the road by the trees. She stood for a minute, judging her best path around this new obstacle. Reddish outcroppings of volcanic rock would make the path difficult at best.

A sudden realisation dawned on her. This must be the lake that Madame de Briand had described—what had she called it? With a clutch of chill Dell remembered. *Le Lac de l'Homme Perdu.* The lake of the lost man.

Yet she had said it was beautiful, and it was. Under the heavy metallic grey of the sky it was impossible to see any signs of the so-called sunken city. But the place had a wild forsaken beauty, a quiet magnificence unspoiled by the hand of man, a splendid isolation. From here, deep in the valley, the town of Saint-Just was no longer visible.

There was nothing for it but to go around the lake. The ground, level here beneath the trees, grew rocky and jagged on the far edges of the water, but it could be managed. Dell veered to the right and held close to the edge of the lake.

The path was easier than it had appeared to be from the distance, and she scrambled nimbly over the rocks, gathering confidence as she progressed. She'd have to hurry now: Saint-Just was at least half an hour from here, and goodness knows when the train came through. Besides, the storm looked as though it were about to break.

'Damn!' The word rang out, and echoed back at her mockingly in the stillness of the valley. Her foot had slipped into a small crevice in the rock. She yanked it fiercely and nothing happened. Well, if the foot had managed to get in there, it must be able to come out. More slowly, she angled the foot first this way, then that, seeking to find the perfect position of exit.

Nothing. This would take some working at. Gingerly, she contorted her body into a sitting position and came to rest on one of the surrounding boulders. There was a groaning shift of the rock and ...

Now the foot was *really* trapped. Her weight had disturbed the boulder slightly, ever so slightly, but enough to change its precarious position. Now the ankle was pinned uncomfortably from all sides, and the slightest movement sent shooting pains up through the leg.

'Damn, damn, damn!' The words sounded like a repeating shotgun against the empty hills, their echo dying away long after Dell had clamped her teeth grimly over the last syllable. She would *not* cry. She would *not*.

There was nothing for it but to try and ease the boulder away from her foot. But that was easier said than done. After all, she was sitting on the rock now, with her foot trapped so securely she couldn't even turn around to get any leverage. She balanced herself on her free foot and, leaning forward as best she could, tried to push the rock backwards. It wouldn't budge.

'Damn!' She clenched her teeth over the word. Perhaps some *paysan* would happen by soon, seeking his cows in the distant fields. She tried to shout for help, but her words only echoed back at her from the surrounding hills. There was nothing to do but wait.

A few fat raindrops fell on her arm and the beginnings of thunder rumbled in the distance. At least she could be looking for some kind of protection from the downpour that was sure to come, and very soon. Lowering herself cautiously on the rock—damn that ankle!—she reached for her handbag which had dropped with the impact, almost beyond her grasp. But she managed to hook a finger around the shoulder strap and draw it towards herself.

Thank goodness for the sweater! It would be soaked through soon enough, but for a time it would absorb the worst of the rain. She dumped the contents of her purse on the rock, looking for something else that might be useful in her present predicament. There was a plastic rain-scarf and she tied it around her head for the little good it would do. Other than that there was nothing. Nothing, nothing!

It was then, with a gigantic clap of thunder, that the rain started in earnest.

CHAPTER ELEVEN

A MIST lay over the morning. Wisps of it rose from the lake, trailing over the motionless surface of the waters. Sometimes it changed into unearthly shapes.

Dell wondered whether her mind was playing tricks. Perhaps there was no mist at all. The night, that endless night, had brought a procession of hallucinations. Perhaps these swirling mists were mere driftings of the imagination that seemed to cease only when a violent fit of shuddering racked her body, jarring her back to the actuality of bone and flesh and skin.

She tried to grasp at straws of sanity, fastening her mind on small solitary things; the shape of a rock, the passage of a beetle, the bend of a blade of grass. But it was too much effort, and she closed her eyes achingly. How long had she been here? A day? Two days? An eternity?

First there had been the storm. Rain, a driving torrent of it, loosed from a vengeful sky. And she remembered the thunder cracking explosively; the lightning flashing as though all the rage of the gods had been loosed upon the little gully.

That first day, a mighty oak tree had been struck, at the edge of the lake, by the stand of trees she had passed earlier. She had seen it split asunder, with a kind of fascinated terror, as if it were no more than a matchstick.

In time the storm had eased, changing to a steady

cold rain that continued until nightfall. She remembered sleeping fitfully, waking often to a starless sky.
But at least the rain had stopped. Morning had
brought a thin sunshine during the early hours after
dawn, and she had removed the sweater to let the luke-
warm rays dry her soaked dress. But a thick cloud
cover had moved in again, heavy with the promise
of more rain, and once more she had huddled her
shoulderblades beneath the cold leaden weight of the
wet sweater.

Hunger had become a problem, too. How long had
it been since Ernestine had offered her a picnic lunch
of rabbit pâté and chicken? But at least she had managed to slake her thirst with the little pools of water
that had collected in depressions of rock.

It had rained again later during the second day, a
thin relentless drizzle that lacked the elemental violence of the storms of the day before. But this was
almost worse. The cold seemed to creep insidiously
into the pores of her skin, into the marrow of her
bones. It plastered her dress to her contours like a
soaked handkerchief, numbed her fingers and feet,
drenched her hair and dragged it across her face, washing clammy wisps into the corners of her mouth and
into her eyes. The plastic rain-scarf had long since been
lost, falling beyond reach on the far side of the rock.

Everything was wet, except her mouth, which felt
cracked and dry, in spite of the water that coursed
down and trickled against the blistered surface of her
lips. Her tongue felt dry, too, dry and stiff and swollen
from vain cries for help. Even during the night when a
ghostly parade of apparitions had moved through the
black curtain of drizzle, Dell had found the will to cry

to them, to call faintly and failingly through the darkness in a voice grown hoarse and parched with effort. But no more.

The strength had long since gone from her voice and from her fingers. It had been hours since she had made any sort of effort to wring out the sweater that had been her one sodden defence against the pervasive wetness of everything. Now it lay over her hunched shoulders, heavy with moisture.

At times she had lost consciousness altogether. The first time this had happened she had slipped from her sitting position on the rock, and the sickening lurch of pain had restored her to instant consciousness. After that she had managed to huddle her body over her trapped foot, curling uncomfortably into an almost foetal position, knees drawn to her chest and head slumped over her arms.

Now mirages were teasing her mind again, as the mist swirled around. Suddenly there was a jumble of shouts, a din of voices echoing in the empty reaches of the rock-strewn valley. This time the hallucinations had a new dimension—sound.

And a shape appeared in the likeness of Raoul. The vision emerged from the mist, looming larger as it closed in from the distance. She slipped into unconsciousness again, gratefully, escaping this final cruelty of the mind.

'Dell!' The sound pulled her back to consciousness. The vision had a voice now, and fingers. The fingers moved over her shoulders, shaking her back to reality, seizing her arms, cupping her head and pulling it against a roughness of cloth that seemed to be his jacket. It was strange how real this delusion seemed:

how solid and dimensional, how reassuring. She let her cheek rub achingly against the heavy fabric and wished the vision could be true.

'Delilah . . .' The voice was Raoul's, sounding hoarse and urgent. Arms enfolded her, protective and passionate, strong and tender.

Then there were other voices. Other hands, not Raoul's, reached down to explore the rock that held her trapped. Someone pushed a stout stick into the crevice, levering at the large stone, sending twinges of pain through her ankle and up her leg. The vision that was Raoul growled angry words at someone and the pain receded. There was a shouting and a shifting of men and something heavy moved. The pressure eased. Then she felt Raoul's fingers again, exquisitely gentle on the agony that was her ankle, and she was free.

Something warm and heavy was pulled around her, covering the sodden, clinging skin of her dress, and the arms encircled her again, pulling her away from the rock. His face was very close, his breath warm against her skin. A delicious languor stole through her limbs, and she nestled close in the haven of his arms.

She touched a swollen tongue to her lips, trying to voice the words that spilled from her heart, but no words came. Raoul pulled her closer against his chest, so close she could feel the beating of his heart. It was strange that he should be wearing only a thin shirt in this weather. Then she realised that his jacket encircled her own shoulders, and she tried to protest, but the effort robbed her of her strength. She closed her eyes and consciousness receded again.

She woke minutes later to another spasm of violent shuddering and the small panicky sense that she had dreamed it all. But he was still there, holding her tightly. His head was bent low to hers now, buried against her neck, the rasp of his unshaven jaw roughly comforting against her cheek.

Gradually the shuddering stopped. Then his head bent close to hers again and she could feel his lips stirring against the wetness of her hair, breathing something low and soothing in her ear.

They were in a car now and someone else was driving. A little strength returnd to her fingers and they stole to his neck, clinging to the collar of his shirt.

The car rocked to a halt. Then she was being carried out of it, still closed in his arms. She could see the château swimming in her vision. There was a flutter of white, which might be Ernestine, the sounds of voices; and she was being carried up the stairs, down the dim corridor, and through a door, still cradled in the curve of Raoul's arms.

The room had a familiar look and she realised that it was her own. Over her ear somewhere, Raoul was barking orders at Ernestine. Ernestine was turning back sheets, laying out blankets, plumping pillows, rummaging through a chest of drawers for something warm.

And Raoul was lowering her gently to the bed. Dell clung to his shirt. He was going to put her down, leave her to Ernestine's care. His hands were on hers, prying them loose from his collar. But he didn't leave her after all. He folded her loosened fingers in his own and she relaxed again.

Then Ernestine was back, and a bundle of towels. More murmurings, and Ernestine reached competent hands forward as if to strip the drenched clothes from

Dell's sodden figure. In the mists of consciousness Dell could hear her crisp words of dismissal to Raoul, and the ring of Raoul's retreating footsteps. Panic seized her and she tried to call to his receding figure, but no words came.

Then Ernestine's hands were on her, raising her from the pillows, pulling away the thin wet fabric of her dress, finding the zipper and freeing it, peeling the drenched garment from her skin and discarding it on the floor. A scattering of flimsy undergarments followed, and Ernestine was towelling her naked skin and pulling a nightgown over her head.

Then, as suddenly as he had left, Raoul was back. Dell felt his arms supporting her gently while Ernestine finished her ministrations. He lowered her against the pillow but did not leave. Panic subsided. Mirage or reality, Raoul was here, and the nearness of him brought weak tears to eyes that Dell had believed could shed no more.

Lean strong fingers moved to her face, lightly brushing away the moisture that had gathered in the corners of her eyes. Then, still wet with tears, the fingers gently traced the hollows and hills of her cheek, a feather touch so light and elusive it might have been another fantasy of her fevered brain. The fingers travelled to her lips, trailing very slowly over the dry blistered surface of them and moving on, vanishing into the still-damp tangle of her hair, soothing and smoothing it against the pillow.

Then her senses numbed and blackness closed in.

CHAPTER TWELVE

THE walls were close, very close now, which was strange, because only moments ago they had been so far away. Then they were receding again, changing shape as they vanished into remoteness. There was a spell of blackness, but not total blackness, for little points of colour flamed into the black and burst into a thousand fragments, like a fireworks display seen at too-close quarters, causing the head to reel and the eyes to burn and the mind to pray for release.

There were faces, too, sometimes. They came and went without rhyme or reason. The face of Raoul, hair a little too long and tousled where he had run angry fingers through it ... Ernestine, starched and sharp-eyed with concern, worried about something, as usual ... then someone large and masculine that might have been her uncle, but it wasn't her uncle, for the face changed to Raoul's again, eyes dark and hollow and a frown furrowing his brow, but the mouth was kind. Once, also, there was Madame de Briand, a ghostly whisper of an image.

And Raoul, always Raoul. Sometimes she squeezed her lids and she could see his eyes seething with fury, or cold with disdain, or glinting with those little gold flecks of sardonic humour ... then the flecks would fragment again, another display of pyrotechnics in the blackness.

Sometimes he swam into vision with such life-like

clarity that he seemed to be real, and there was no
anger or scorn or laughter in his eyes, only a terrible
haunted look, and Dell longed to reach her fingers out
to touch his face and comfort him. But her fingers
weren't there, she was sure: she tried to move them
and nothing happened. Maybe they were somebody
else's fingers.

When she woke, the sun was shining, streaming in the
window and sifting its warmth through the curtains.

'Mademoiselle?' said someone, very softly, and Dell
turned her head—the effort made it ache—to find the
voice. It was Ernestine, and Dell tried to smile at her,
but her mouth was too parched. Instead she touched a
tongue to her lips, running it with an effort over skin
that felt strange and dry. Then Ernestine was wiping
her face with a cool damp cloth, and easing her shoulders upward to hold a small glass of water to her lips.
The few drops of liquid gave Dell a measure of
strength, and she essayed a smile again—this time with
a little more success.

But the effort was enormous. She closed her eyes and
slept again.

In her dream Raoul came once more, so real, so near
that she could feel the touch of him—the warmth of
his hands, cupping hers with infinite gentleness; the
soft fanning of his breath against her cheek. She tried
to grasp the vision, but there was no strength in her
fingers; to turn her face towards the whisper of his
mouth, but her body refused to obey her brain. Instead there was only a sense of powerlessness. Then the
dream was gone. Or had it been a dream?

When she opened her eyes, finally, it was to the

ministrations of Ernestine. Ernestine was urging some
clear broth to her lips. It seemed that Ernestine was
always worried about everybody's stomach. Dell would
have liked to smile, but instead the merest twitch
flickered across her lips.

'Mademoiselle is much better today,' proclaimed
Ernestine decisively, and because Ernestine said it Dell
knew it must be true. Although she didn't feel much
better.

The broth was a restorative and Dell sipped at the
cup slowly and gratefully. She would have liked more,
but Ernestine firmly set the cup aside and told her she
would have to wait. Too much at one time would not
be good for Mademoiselle. The fever, after all, had
broken only yesterday. Mademoiselle had been very ill,
and it would be another day before she could return to
a proper diet. The exposure, after all.

'How long——' Dell still found speech difficult.

'Mademoiselle has had the fever for four days now.'
Ernestine smoothed the sheet and adjusted Dell's hands
to a more comfortable position. 'Madame has been very
worried about you—but yesterday, the doctor says the
time for alarm has passed.'

'And Raoul . . . ?'

'It is Monsieur Raoul who has found you, finally.' So
it had been Raoul. That much had not been a figment
of her tortured imagination. 'But it was a matter of
two days. The men, they were looking in the other
direction, towards La Chaise Dieu. *Eh bien*, you must
not trouble your head with these thoughts! You must
rest now and when you wake, more broth.'

It took little urging, for Dell's eyes were already
closing and she slid easily into a deep, dreamless sleep

that lasted for several hours. When she woke again it
was nearly dark. Ernestine still sat beside the bed, holding a lonely vigil in the gathering gloom. When she saw
that Dell had wakened, she reached over to switch on
a bedside lamp.

'Ernestine! You should be with Madame de Briand,'
murmured Dell with concern.

'No, *mademoiselle*. Madame has told me I am to remain with you until you are recovered.'

'But who is looking after her?' Dell thought of
Eugénie de Briand in her darkness, deprived of the
woman who had become her eyes. The thought brought
a tremble to her lips, and she felt a tear roll unchecked
down the side of her nose. It was this appalling weakness, she told herself.

'Mademoiselle is not to worry. Héloise is a good girl;
she has been looking after Madame. But now you have
passed the crisis, and I will be returning to her tonight.
Eh bien, you must have some broth to restore the
strength, *n'est-ce pas?*'

Ernestine offered not only broth, but a small tray of
food which appeared at the door carried by Marie-Ange
herself. The plain, proud woman mirrored Ernestine's
look of concern. It was flattering how everybody seemed
to be so worried about her, thought Dell weakly; everybody except the one person she wanted to see now more
than anyone else in the world.

There was a soft-boiled egg and a small plate of but-
tered toast fingers, as well as a freshly-made pot of weak
tea. At Ernestine's insistence Dell managed to eat a
creditable amount. Then she lay back against her
pillows, exhausted.

With her eyes closed, she tried to remember what

had happened. The drive towards Saint-Just-sur-Haute was clear enough, and the hiding of the car. Then the descent into the gully, sans shoes and pantyhose. She could still remember with horror the sensation of being imprisoned, her ankle paining her fiercely when she tried to move, that animal panic that must come to free wild creatures when the trap springs. She could almost feel the rain, first soft and warm, then pelting ferociously with such stinging force that it seemed like a liquid battering ram.

Then the nightmare unreality of that second night, when even hunger had passed and her mind had started to wander. Dell felt beads of sweat forming on her upper lip at the mere remembrance of it.

And the rescue. Raoul's face, Raoul's hands, Raoul's arms, arms that had been like a homecoming after a dangerous voyage, like a safe haven in a storm. Beyond that she remembered little more than flashes: will-o'-the-wisp memories that flickered at the edges of her mind, defying her efforts to grasp them.

And where was Raoul now? Here at Montperdu—or in Paris?

She stirred restlessly in the bed, and Ernestine leaned over to plump her pillows to a more comfortable position.

Another day passed before Dell found enough strength to stay awake for more than an hour or two at a time. Ernestine no longer maintained her bedside vigil, but Héloise came frequently to tend to her needs. The local doctor came, too. Doctor Charlevoix, from the village of Saint-Just-sur-Haute, was a gruff grey portly man, and Dell liked him immediately.

At Madame de Briand's insistence, Ernestine

brought her to Dell's bedside. It must have taken a great effort of will on the part of the older woman. Dell thought she looked very ill and very old, as though she too had been through a time of crisis, this woman who had once seemed so magnificent in the beauty of her age. The visit was a short one, no more than a few minutes, and Ernestine soon led Madame de Briand away, before Dell found herself able to convey anything of the regrets that plagued her.

Of Raoul there was still no sign. Had he been at Montperdu, at her bedside, since the rescue? Or had she imagined it? The latter, she decided. Raoul would have left for Paris long ago: probably soon after he had returned her to safety. As it was, she thought ruefully, she must have caused him endless trouble and delay on the eve of his show.

The following day she was allowed out of bed. It had been an odd rubbery feeling at first, but gradually the strength returned to her limbs and within two more days she felt almost totally restored. Doctor Charlevoix came again, twice, and on his last visit pronounced her much improved.

'You are a healthy young woman, fortunately,' the doctor clucked at her, easing his ponderous weight on to a chair beside her bed. 'I just wish that Eugénie de Briand had your recuperative powers.'

'She does seem rather ill,' reflected Dell remorsefully, wondering how much she herself had contributed to Madame de Briand's poor health.

'An illness of the spirit,' the doctor murmured. 'A diagnosis I am also tempted to make for you.'

'I'm feeling a hundred per cent now,' demurred Dell. 'I was downstairs for dinner last night, and I spent this morning walking in the sunshine.'

'Not a hundred per cent, entirely,' disagreed the doctor, with a lowering of his heavy grey brows. 'There is something troubling you, I think.'

'Nothing,' lied Dell with an attempt at a smile, 'except that I'd like to be at home with my aunt and uncle. I haven't seen them for so long——' She found her chin trembling slightly. It wasn't what she wanted at all.

'It can be arranged,' said the doctor gravely. 'You can travel soon, perhaps two, three days. I will speak to Madame de Briand. But you must stop this—this eating of the insides. There are some things even we doctors cannot cure.'

There were indeed things the doctors couldn't cure. Raoul, like a fever in her brain, a sickness of the soul. She had tried to exorcise him from her mind but he wouldn't go.

By now Dell was certain he must have gone to Paris. The question had burned on the tip of her tongue a thousand times. But Dell had been too proud to ask, afraid that some traitorous expression would betray the inner turmoil of her emotions. Ernestine seemed to take his absence for granted and apparently it didn't occur to her to mention the matter to Dell.

It wasn't until she saw Madame de Briand again that she learned, with certainty, of Raoul's whereabouts.

Doctor Charlevoix had forbidden the failing woman to hazard any more excursions from her room, so it was there that Dell visited her. She was shocked by the deterioration in Madame de Briand's appearance, even in the two days since she had seen her. The older woman was visibly declining. Her skin seemed shrunken across her sculpted cheekbones, investing the face with an almost spiritual quality, as if she were merely an older version of the Madonna that graced her walls. It was as though her once-proud face were withering into a death-mask of itself. Dell's heart ached with pity and regret for the pain she had caused the other woman.

'I—hoped you wouldn't mind if I came to see you.' Dell smiled tremulously at the wraith-like figure that sat huddled in the rocking chair. Ernestine had vanished for the moment, closing the door silently behind her.

'I should have been distraught if you had not.' Madame de Briand let a ghost of a smile play over her face. 'Ernestine tells me you are much improved.'

'I am.' A small awkward silence followed, then Dell spoke in a rush of words. 'I don't know how to say this, but—nothing I ever did was intended to hurt you. I wouldn't——' her voice broke a little, '—wouldn't have hurt you for worlds. Somehow I've had the feeling during these past weeks that you really were—family. If you had been my mother—mother-in-law—I couldn't have been prouder. I don't like to think that I've made you suffer so.'

Madame de Briand sighed heavily. 'Did you? I think not. One punishes oneself sometimes. The matter about Rhys—that I could forget, have forgotten. But the thought that you might have died and it would have been I who had killed you! If I had not spoken to you that night as I did ...'

'That's not true!' Dell broke in with a warm denial. 'There were other—other things that made me feel I must go. It wasn't—you.' She longed to explain further, but could not. She studied her hands unhappily. What more could she say to Madame de Briand without revealing her love for Raoul?

The other woman sat in silence for a moment, as if mulling over Dell's enigmatic remark. When she spoke again it was almost as if to herself, as though she were groping her way through a maze of understanding. 'Other ... ? Then——'

She fell silent again and Dell spoke hastily, afraid that she might somehow have betrayed the truth of her emotions. 'Doctor Charlevoix says I may go home in two days. I—I hope you won't mind.'

'Yes, I mind.' Eugénie de Briand sighed and shifted in her chair. 'Raoul will mind too. He was most concerned about you when he left, and had the doctor not told him you had passed the danger point ...'

Dell sat wordlessly, scarcely daring to move, hoping Madame de Briand would say more yet afraid to hear what she might say.

The explanation continued. 'But Raoul was already several days late in going to Paris. The people in Paris, they were nearly beside themselves. The show could not be delayed, you understand.'

'I wouldn't have expected him to do anything else,' said Dell in a small voice. So Raoul *had* been at Montperdu in the days following the accident.

'He will be back in one more week.' Madame de Briand paused for a moment, expectantly, as if listening for invisible vibrations in the air.

'I'm sure it will be a successful show.' Dell tried to keep the strain from telling in her voice. 'I'll look forward to—reading about it in the papers.'

'Perhaps it would be best if you stayed on for a

while,' said Madame de Briand with apparent careless-
ness. 'Raoul has been very concerned for your health.
He has been phoning every day—twice, three times a
day. This, for a man who scorns the telephone ...'

Dell dropped her head over a clenched fist, squeezing
her eyes to restrain the sudden tears that stabbed at the
back of her eyes. So he had been phoning every day.
Yet he had never asked to speak to *her* ... probably it
was a natural solicitude for his mother that had
prompted the calls. It was true that the mists of
memory told her that Raoul had been concerned during those first terrible days after the accident. Of course
he had been concerned! He might have been equally
concerned had it been Ernestine or Marie-Ange or
Gaspard who had been in such a plight.

At length she found her voice. 'Then you can tell
him—tell him I'm fine.'

'Why do you not wait and tell him yourself?'

'I—I'd like to be home with my aunt and uncle.
My—my aunt has arranged to meet me in Paris, the day
after tomorrow, so I won't be—entirely alone for the
trip.'

Eugénie de Briand pursed her lips and frowned, as
though thinking that over. Finally: 'As you wish. But
before you leave, my child,' she finished, settling back
into the chair, 'come and see me again.'

Dell had seen her once again, last night. It was a
poignant moment, washed—for Dell at least—with the
bitter memories of what had been. She felt her throat
heavy with the knowledge that she would not see
Madame de Briand again. Yet she was relieved to see
that the older woman seemed curiously calm, as if she
had reached some sort of peace with herself. Perhaps

she no longer blamed herself for the accident. There was even a faint warmth of colour in her aged cheeks, and she seemed rather stronger than she had the day before.

Now all was in readiness for the departure. Dell cast a farewell look around her room. She would miss Montperdu. Lost mountain ... a symbol of all the things she was losing, without ever having had them in her grasp.

The days of recuperation had brought some of the flesh back to her cheeks, but not the warm glow of colour, the fire that had once shone from her eyes. She felt strong enough now to undertake the trip home, but there was a listlessness that had not been there before. Fortunately Gaspard and Ernestine had made all the travel arrangements for her. Now there was only the waiting.

Restlessly, she re-checked her bureau drawers, the bathroom, the armoire, to see if anything had been left behind. Nothing ... only the lace blouse, which she had retrieved from a forgotten corner and hung carefully on a hanger in the armoire. She let her fingers glide lightly over the texture of the sleeve. But it reminded her too much of Raoul's touch, and she turned away with an aching sense of emptiness.

The suitcases stood ready by the door. Gaspard would carry them to the car when it was time to go. There was only one thing she hadn't packed: the red sweater, worn so long ago, that she had left inadvertently in Raoul's studio. She had not liked to ask Ernestine for the key. It would have to be sent to her, later.

She had said her farewells to Marie-Ange and Ernestine this morning, sorry to be leaving them, yet absurdly comforted to see the fat tear that Ernestine wiped away with one crisp corner of her apron. How different from her last departure!

It would be at least an hour before Gaspard would bring the Renault to the front door of the château. Only a few minutes ago, she thought she had heard the car revving outside, but when she had checked through the slit of window in the hallway outside her bedroom, there had been no sign of Gaspard, or of the Renault.

Outside the day was golden, far too fine a day to spend closeted with regrets for what could never be. Dell decided to wait on the front steps of the château. She walked downstairs, slowly, letting her fingers caress the patina of wood on the banisters, letting her eyes devour, for one last time, the peaceful courtyard sleeping in the summer warmth. The house held memories, too many memories. She turned away and, opening the creaking front door, emerged into the sun.

Strange, the door of the studio—Raoul's studio— was ajar. Ernestine and Héloïse must be giving it a good cleaning in his absence. Perhaps she could retrieve the red sweater after all. It would save Ernestine having to send it.

She walked across the courtyard irresolutely, and paused at the door of the studio, half expecting to find a bustle of activity inside. But there was nothing, nobody, only the empty sun-washed interior, and silence. Neither Ernestine nor Héloïse was in sight.

Most of the canvases that had lined the walls were gone, as she had expected they would be. A few small paintings, and some raw canvas on stretchers, stood against one wall; and one large painting remained on the easel at the far side of the room, hidden from view. The portrait of Noëlle, probably. Dell wrenched her gaze away from it.

She could see the flash of red across the room, her sweater, carelessly draped across the long workbench. She moved across the space as if in suspension, scarcely daring to breathe lest the stirring should awaken slumbering memories.

'Dell!'

The voice hit her like a physical blow, a shock of recognition, and her hand pulled away from the sweater as if scalded.

She whirled around to face Raoul. He stood in the doorway, easily, a tentative smile tugging crookedly at the corners of his mouth. Her heart lurched guiltily, taking a plummet over the precipice of a roller-coaster. Then the sensation passed.

Raoul stepped into the room and clicked the door behind him. For a moment he moved no closer, only stood there, regarding her across the space with that small smile and eyes that seemed watchful, expectant, curiously glittering.

He was still dressed in his travelling clothes. Dell tore her eyes away, for the memories came tumbling back too swiftly at the sight of him.

'I—I came for my sweater,' she stumbled, eyes seemingly transfixed by a plank that stood against the wall somewhere beyond his right shoulder. But she could still see him. He had started to move towards her now. She could feel rather than see his eyes upon her and she knew how they would look—heavy-lidded, the indigo-purple of the volcanic Auvergnian mountains, with little molten flecks of gold swimming in their depths. He was coming close, too close.

She kept her face averted. 'I thought you were in Paris.'

'I was. I got back just a few minutes ago.' He paused for the moment and came to a halt mere inches away from her: so close she could feel her pulse grow turbulent with the warmth of his body and the good soap-clean smell of him. She quelled the desire to move closer, to bury her head against the breadth of his chest. Little warning signals tingled along her nerve endings, and she retreated a step, involuntarily.

Raoul lifted a hand, as if to touch her, then dropped it again, with visible effort. 'I thought I'd find you inside. In the house.'

'I—came down, because I—I'm leaving today. In about an hour. I'm m-meeting my aunt, in Paris.' Dell's lips felt stiff and inadequate to the task of maintaining any semblance of formality.

'Are you?' Raoul spoke very softly. 'I think not. You shouldn't be travelling yet.'

'The doctor said I could go.' Dell half-turned away from him, a defensive gesture, to let her shoulder serve as a small protective barrier against the enormity of his presence.

'And you would have gone—just like that? Without a goodbye?'

She looked down at her hands, trying to will away the trembling that had seized them. 'I said goodbye to your mother.'

'So she told me, yesterday.'

'I didn't think you'd—care. You could have said goodbye on the phone.'

'The phone is no place to say goodbye.'

'Well then——' the words seemed lame, clumsy, '—goodbye. And—thank you.'

'Thank you?'

'For—for saving my life.'

'You can thank Noëlle for that. If she hadn't——' There was a heavy note of sarcasm in his voice, and he left the sentence unfinished. Dell felt a knot of unpleasantness at the base of her throat. She didn't want to owe anything to Noëlle.

'I'm sure you voiced the appropriate sentiments for me.' The trembling had stopped now; her hands were under control.

'I did.' His voice was abrupt, dismissive, but she could feel his eyes still on her, lingering.

Dell cleared her throat. 'You were—late getting off for Paris, on account of me. I'm sorry.'

'Paris be damned!'

Dell felt her knuckles whiten with the effort of self-control, but she managed to keep her voice light. 'Did the critics like your show?'

Raoul gave a soft amused laugh. 'I don't know. It doesn't open until tonight.'

She darted a look at him then, swiftly, and returned her eyes to the neutrality of space straight ahead of her. 'But you'll——'

'Miss it?' Raoul shrugged, as if it was of little consequence. 'I never liked openings anyway.'

'So that's why you—came back.'

'You know why I came back, Dell.' His voice roughened, taking on a thick timbre, and Dell felt something flop inside her, a swift strange sensation, almost a pain, somewhere in the pit of her stomach.

'Do I?'

The question hung between them, a whisper that seemed to loom large in the silence of the room. Then Raoul's hand rose and touched her arm, lightly. He was urging her across the room, gently, drawing her towards the large easel that stood with its back to the door, canvas propped against the inverted vee of the frame, just as it had been weeks before when she had first seen it.

There was a weak resistance in her fingers. She didn't want to see the portrait of Noëlle, not now, not ever.

'Maybe this will help you understand.' He pulled her, unwilling but unable to withstand his insistent grasp, into the bath of sunlight that fell over the finished portrait.

It was not a portrait of Noëlle after all. Dell stared uncomprehendingly at the canvas, and the face that stared back at her was her own.

It was all there: the fiery tumble of golden auburn hair, pulled carelessly behind the ears, with a trail of soft tendrils about the face. The eyes, as he had once described them, wide-spaced and looking outward, level and grave and grey, as though they saw something the rest of the world did not see. The generous mouth, too wide by far, but soft and just barely opened with a breathless, hushed, tremulous expectancy. The chin: you could almost see the beginnings of a quiver in the skill of the artist's brush, the hint of defiance in the tilt of the bone.

And the portrait that stared back at Dell was wearing the blouse. The lace blouse. It plunged over skin creamy and soft as a baby's, a gentle swell of breast that spoke of newly ripened womanhood, sensuous yet pure,

a tender tribute that could have only been painted
by ...

'Fire and innocence,' murmured Raoul very softly,
and Dell turned to face him with a wakening wonder
in her eyes.

'You love me,' she said, a statement of fact, not a
question.

'I think I always have,' he answered simply, 'but I
didn't know it. It took the canvas to tell me.'

'But you said nothing,' whispered Dell, her hands
very still against her breast—so still, she could feel the
rhythm of her heart. 'I thought you were painting a
portrait of Noëlle.'

'I was.' Raoul made no move to close the small distance between them. But his eyes touched her, moved
over her, a caress as intimate as skin-on-skin. 'It told me
everything I needed to know about Noëlle. I couldn't
finish it.'

'I don't suppose she liked that.'

'Noëlle be hanged! She didn't like a lot of things I
told her. Anyone who could keep silent for so long,
knowing the car was——' His eyes clouded, stormy suddenly, and he failed to finish his sentence, almost as
though the words had stuck in his throat. 'But I'd had
it out with Noëlle before that. The night she came to
dinner.'

'And that note she sent——'

'A final plea, that was all. Noëlle was—finished long
ago.'

'Oh.' Dell inspected her fingers, half reluctant to let
even the smallest thoughts of the other woman intrude
on the joy that welled up inside her—yet, woman-like,
wanting to know, once and for all; to wipe the slate

clean and finish with Noëlle for ever.

'Noëlle was never important to me—not really. But I can't deny that she—existed. I'm a man,' he shrugged.

'I've noticed.' Dell smiled tremulously and let her eyes travel upward again, under thick lashes, to seek and devour the dear contours of his face. 'Oh, Raoul ...'

With a groan, he gathered her into his arms, his lips reaching hungrily for hers.

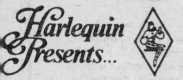